D0772545

MISADVENTURES OF A
MAGICIAN'S SON

written and illustrated by
Laurie Smollett Kutscera

BLUE WHALE PRESS

Misadventures of a Magician's Son

Text and illustrations copyright © 2020 by Laurie Smollett Kutscera

Published by Blue Whale Press LLC, U.S.A.
All rights reserved.

No part of this book may be reproduced or transmitted by any means, either mechanical or electronic, or stored in a retrieval system, or otherwise copied for public or private use without obtaining prior permission from the publisher in writing except as allowed under "fair use", which permits quotations embodied in critical articles or reviews.

Visit us at www.bluewhalepress.com, or contact us by sending email to:
info@bluewhalepress.com

Address all inquiries to:
Blue Whale Press, 237 Rainbow Dr. #13702, Livingston, TX 77399

Publisher's Cataloging-in-Publication data available upon request

Library of Congress Control Number: 2019932900

ISBN: 978-1-7328935-4-2 (hardcover)
ISBN: 978-1-7328935-3-5 (paperback)
ISBN: 978-1-7328935-5-9 (e-book)

To my husband, Nick,

I am forever grateful. Your patience, support and encouragement have meant everything to me. Thank you for bringing magic into our lives.

—LSK

A very special thank you: To an exceptional critique group led by Kate McKean at Media Bistro in NYC. Melissa, Jeff, Fran, Jess, Colin, Samantha and Kate—working with you all has been the highlight of my writing journey.

To Lucy Van Hoff, a most passionate middle grade librarian and dear friend, for sharing this marvelous genre with me and for introducing me to the work of Kate DiCamillo.

To John Logigian who after reading umpteen million screenplays, still found the light in my first draft.

To Kyle Majid for his lacrosse expertise.

To Braedan Scarlatos, Christopher Wolfe, Bob Johnson, Stacey Lancaster, and Enid Logigian for being the perfect models. Each one of these characters came to life with your help.

A most heartfelt thank you to Joel Goldman, magician extraordinaire. Joel was 16 when I began writing this novel. He spent endless hours showing me his array of perfectly polished card tricks and illusions. He answered hundreds of questions and allowed me to take photographs and videos of his remarkable fingers in action. Today, he still practices magic when he's not traveling the world.

CONTENTS

SPECIAL DELIVERY

Alexander Finn yanked his hood over his head and slipped behind the old oak tree. He hid there watching the afternoon school bus loaded with twitchy middle graders pull away from the curb. Spitballs in full launch, the bus turned the corner, and Alex ran off in the opposite direction.

He had wandered the cobblestone streets for nearly an hour when the fog pushed through. Backpack flung over his shoulder, he charged ahead. His eyes fixed on the ominous cloud as it crept up the hill from the harbor and brushed against his legs. It was as if the damp, ghostly form had a mind of its own.

Once he reached his weathered-gray, clapboard house with emptied cartons piled upon the porch, Alex stopped short and let the fog catch up to him. In a flash, he was lost in a bittersweet memory of his father draped in black, high above the footlights. His arms were raised to the heavens and his legs stretched wide as white vapor coiled from both sides of the stage. The audience roared with applause. Alex dropped his backpack and raised his arms. He closed his eyes and let the fog envelop him.

"Not too bright stoppin' in the middle of the street like that, young man," a gruff voice snapped behind him.

Alex jumped aside. "Oh! . . . Sorry." He could just make out the large piece of furniture the man was lugging through the dense fog. He tried to touch it when a shorter man grasping the other end pushed it through the mist and up the front porch before he had the chance.

"Watch that step," the gruff man said.

"Yeah, I got it," the shorter man grumbled.

Alex stayed close behind as they struggled up the rickety stairway to his bedroom on the second floor. The house was small. Much smaller than the house he had spent his first twelve years in. His new room, still piled high with unpacked boxes, seemed more like a closet than a bedroom. The newly-moved desk now looked like a large truck parked in the middle of it. His mother had planned to sell it, but Alex wouldn't hear of it. That piece meant everything to him.

Once the van drove off, Alex and his mom stood in his doorway gazing at the old desk smothered in plastic.

"Maybe they should have left this in the living room," she said.

Alex jumped in front of her. "It's fine right here!"

His mom stepped around him. "Did you make the bus this morning?"

Alex hesitated. "Almost."

"What about this afternoon?"

Alex rolled his eyes. He had no desire to sit on a bus with a bunch of weirdo kids he didn't know. Why couldn't he just walk home? After another school day filled with questions from prying teachers and gossipy students, it was a welcome break to walk alone with nothing but his thoughts. But Alex didn't say a word. Once his mom had her mind made up, she wasn't about to change it—*so why bother?* He just shoved his hands in his pockets and shrugged.

"Alex, please don't make this any harder than it has to be. With everything that's going on right now I can't worry about you wandering the streets or being late for school." She dropped onto the edge of his bed. "It's just us now, and I'm really going to need your help."

Alex folded his arms and leaned against the doorframe. He didn't feel much like helping. After all, it was her idea to move so far away and start in a new school where he didn't know anyone. Did she really expect him to be cheery and helpful?

His mom sat there for a moment, her eyes rising and falling along his box-cluttered wall. "Alright! Now that the last moving van has left, do you think maybe it's time to start unpacking?"

He looked around his tiny room and glared at the towering stack. All his belongings and happier memories—everything that once mattered to him—were now propped up against the wall in cardboard boxes. Alex said nothing. He stepped over to the window and leaned his head against the glass.

His mom got up and placed her hand firmly on his shoulder. "Look, I know this has been difficult, but you do know eventually you're going to have to come to terms with the idea that this is our home now, right?"

Her voice faded into the milky air that draped itself around lampposts and rendered the row of parked cars along the incline invisible. Alex knew there was no way he could ever call this place home. Ridge Park, New York, six hundred and twenty-three miles away, would always be home. That's where his best friend Tyler lived. That's where his lacrosse team and the science club were. That's where his heart was.

His mom turned to leave. "You have until the weekend. Otherwise, I'm bringing in the troops!"

3

Alex gave her a tight smile. At that moment, unpacking boxes was the last thing on his mind. He watched her disappear down the stairs then turned to the desk and began ripping at the layers of bubble wrap.

Fistfuls of torn plastic exposed the dark mahogany and brass trim he had grown to admire. This had been the centerpiece of his father's study. Alex's thoughts wandered back to that sanctuary of illusions where paintings of Houdini and Kellar hung on opposite sides of the fireplace. Rabbit-sized contraptions were stacked on the floor, and books on the subject of magic soared to the ceiling. There were trophies lined up like soldiers and photographs capturing the most dramatic reveals flaunted in every corner.

Alex shoved the bubble wrap aside and grabbed a chair. He sat there for a moment, running his palms across the top of the desk. He laid his cheek down, pressed his ear against its smooth cool surface, and listened. He stayed like that for some time, hoping for a whisper or the faintest tap.

"Dad? Can you hear me? It's Alex," he whispered. But all he heard was the occasional rumble of a car rushing down the street.

He took a deep breath and opened the top drawer. A couple of pencils rolled forward and rested against a magnifying glass. Its handle was made from an elk's antler, and when he peered through the glass, his fingers looked like thick sausages. Inside the drawer, between a scattering of paper clips and rubber bands, lay a photograph in a silver frame. A sad smile grew on Alex's face. The photo had been taken moments after his father had successfully performed The Dance of Suits for the first and only time.

He picked up the frame and studied it in the afternoon light. His own reflection flickered beside his father's image. For a brief moment, it was as if they stood side by side. Alex wiped the smudged frame with the front of his T-shirt and positioned it on the empty desk. It felt good to have his father smiling at him again.

He pulled at the bottom drawer. It wouldn't budge. He braced himself and gave it a yank, but it was locked tight. Alex leaned closer. Just below the handle was a heart-shaped keyhole. But where was the key? He ran his fingers along the inside of the drawers and under the desk until he heard a faint jingle, like a coin dropping to the floor.

He got on his knees and felt around, patting his fingers in circles until he came upon a small brass key dangling from a piece of tape. The key looked like the kind used to open a jewelry box. Alex slid it into the keyhole, and the drawer clicked open.

Certain it would be overflowing with notes and sketches detailing every magic trick his father had performed, he couldn't wait to look inside the drawer. But it was empty. Flecks of dust spun in the shadows. *This makes no sense. Why would Dad lock an empty drawer?* Alex leaned his head inside and squinted into the darkness. Something was tucked deep in the back. He reached in and pulled out a gloss-black lacquered box. It was inlaid with pieces of abalone shell that shimmered in the light. Alex lifted the lid. Inside, he discovered a deck of playing cards.

Alex jumped to his feet. He shook the cards from the box and inspected them a few at a time—turning them over, checking their weight, flexing them gently between his thumb and index finger. He skimmed his fingers across their faces and fanned them into a circle. He divided the deck in two and began to shuffle, his thumbs pressed against their edges. The cards fluttered alternately into a single pile. He shuffled again. With the lightest touch, he spread them across the top of the desk and gently tapped the last one, sending the rest over like a row of dominoes.

"Alex!" his mom screamed from downstairs.

Alex threw the cards on the desk and raced downstairs. He found his mom in the kitchen, leaning at a forty-five-degree angle. She was holding up a cabinet that had come loose from the wall. Broken glass and plates littered the yellowed linoleum floor.

It took a while to clean up the mess. Once they pried the cabinet away, they stood there staring at the faded water stains and rotting timbers.

Alex's mom picked up a shard of her favorite china. "It seems our *classic silver clapboard* might have been code for *rotting gray hovel.*"

They barely spoke a word during dinner, both of them pushing their food around their plates. Alex's eyes kept jumping to the gaping hole in the wall where the cabinet used to be. It all seemed like a bad dream. In her haste to get him settled before the school year started, his mom not only forced him to leave the only home he knew, she also rushed into buying a house— the wrong house! Alex's stomach was in knots. He slid his chair from the table, climbed the creaky stairs to his room, and shut the door.

That night, he lay in bed and listened to the tree outside his window scratch against the old place. Its gnarled shadow swept across the massive pile of unpacked boxes. He thought about his dad and wondered what he would have said about the move to Maine. He thought about how much he missed Tyler and his lacrosse teammates and how his life had changed in ways he didn't even want to consider. Soon, his eyes grew heavy and his thoughts drifted away.

WHACKACKACK! It sounded like a tree had crashed through the roof. Alex shot up, his heart in his throat, his arms and legs flailing as he tried to get his bearings. A constant rattle filled the air as he fumbled for the light. There was no doubt in his mind—the old house was collapsing around him.

An Introduction . . . of Sorts

Alex clutched his chest, relieved it was only the shutters slamming back and forth against his bedroom wall. Chilly autumn air blasted through his room. He jumped out of bed and leaned across the desk to shut the window. That's when he noticed the deck of cards scattered on the floor. Alex had run out in such a hurry when his mom screamed that he'd forgotten to place them back in their abalone box. He dropped to his knees and began scooping them into a pile when he heard a strange snap.

"I'll have you know, this is imported silk you're handling!" a tiny voice barked.

Alex fell backward and hit his head on the corner of his night table. He rubbed his scalp and tried to focus on what appeared to be a four-inch-tall clown feverishly brushing the front of his brightly colored jacket. Clutching his scepter, he glared at Alex then twisted his body as if he were made of rubber.

"How's the back?" he asked. The bells on his tiny hat jingled wildly.

Alex's eyes opened wide. "Uh . . ."

Seconds later, there was another snap.

"Joker!" An equally diminutive woman, wearing a crown of gold, whispered loudly. Her graceful skirt made a swooshing sound as she climbed from the heap of cards and scurried to his side.

"This is *not* how we planned our introduction!"

Alex kept blinking. He had to be dreaming.

At once, there was a third snap. Another card transformed before Alex. This time, a kingly figure appeared. Shoulders back, chest puffed out, he marched across the floor, his red robe billowing in his wake. He tipped his crown at Alex then glared at Joker. "What is wrong with you man?"

Alex's jaw dropped. Before he had a chance to form words, *snap*, a younger man wearing a tiny crown jumped from a card. He gave his legs a shake, as if he had just run a marathon, and then sprinted over to the king and queen. The young man chuckled at the clown with the jangly hat. "Joker, you are definitely, positively a piece of work!"

"This can't be happening!" Alex covered his eyes with his hands. He sat there, praying that when he looked again, they'd all be gone. But when Joker's bells continued to jingle, as if he were a dog with a flea problem, Alex knew this was no dream. He slowly spread his fingers.

There they were, frowning at Joker. All at once, they turned and looked at Alex.

"Yes, well then." The king cleared his throat. He threw his arm in the air, and with a snap of his fingers, the cards strewn behind him transformed into clusters of tiny people, each dressed in the finest regal fashion. They straightened their frocks and robes and inched closer. "I imagine this must be quite a shock," the king added, glancing around him.

Alex nodded slowly.

"Yes, yes, indeed," the king mumbled as he stroked his beard. "Perhaps I should begin by introducing myself. I am King Anton, the King of Hearts. And this is my beloved Olivia, the Queen of Hearts."

Queen Olivia smoothed her hair and curtsied. "How do you do, Alexander? My, you've grown into a handsome young man! You were such a beautiful baby."

"Uh . . . I . . . uh," was all Alex could muster.

"May I also introduce to you our son, Jack?" the King said.

Jack stood there for a moment. His eyes roamed from one corner of the room to the other. The King let out a sigh. He yanked his sword from his sheath and gently nudged his son with it.

Jack stumbled forward. "Oh, uh, hi."

Alex's mouth hung open.

"And here we have the Diamond family," the King said.

The Diamonds stepped forward. Their queen fluttered her lashes and curtsied while their king tossed his robe over his shoulder and bowed. "It is a pleasure to meet you, young man."

"May I present the Spade family," King Anton said.

Just behind the Diamonds, the Spades made their way forward. Their king and queen stepped lightly, circling about as though they had just completed a ballroom dance. "It is a privilege, Alexander," they said as they bowed and backed away.

Alex nodded.

"I should also like to introduce the Club family," King Anton said.

The Clubs jumped through the crowd. Their king and queen waved at Alex then repeatedly bowed and curtsied away in unison. "So delightful to meet you!" They beamed. King Anton marched before them all. He placed his hand over his heart and lowered his head. "As the ambassador of the assembly before you, it truly is an honor, Alexander."

Alex offered the tiniest smile.

"Ummmm . . . hell-ooo!" a rather irritating voice chimed in.

King Anton grimaced. As if preparing to share the worst possible news, he jabbed his sword in the carpet and leaned hard on its hilt. "Oh yes, lest I forget . . . *this* is Joker."

Without a moment's hesitation, Joker stomped forward and threw his hand on his hip. "I'm sure I'm not the first to tell you, but this place is in dire need of a makeover! Seriously. That desk has got to go! I need to talk with someone immediately. Otherwise, Emilio and I are sure to catch pneumonia by that drafty old window." He cradled Emilio, his little scepter, like a baby for Alex to see.

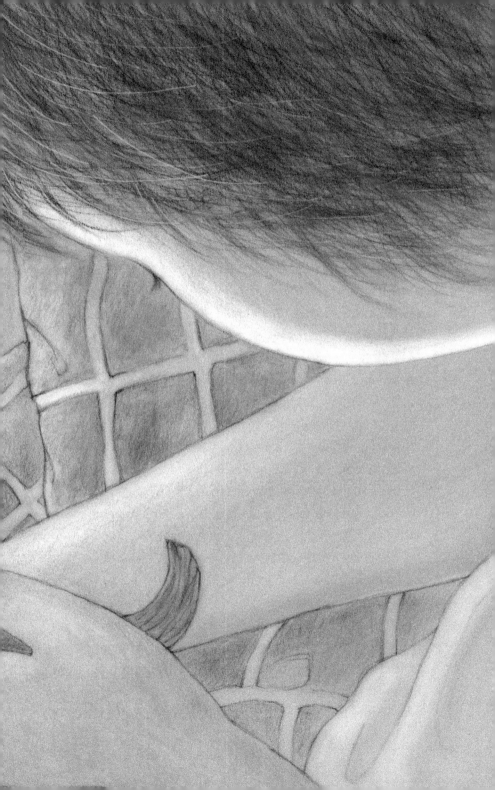

Alex crawled backward. He leaned his head against the massive desk and ran his fingers across the wood grain. "It—it was my father's. I like having it in my room. It feels like he's still with me."

The King stepped closer but sprang back when his sword remained stuck in the carpet. "You don't have to explain a thing, Alex," he said, somewhat distracted as he struggled to pluck the sword free.

"Certainly not!" the Queen agreed. "We understand completely. We knew your father well."

Alex turned to her. "You did?"

King Anton slid his sword in its sheath. He reached beneath his robe and pulled out a glimmering gold pocket watch. He clicked it open and raised his arm toward Alex.

"Your father was a great magician but an even greater friend. We owe our very existence to him."

Alex squinted at the King's tiny hand. He reached down and lifted the watch by its chain. Barely able to make out the image dangling in the cover, he grabbed the magnifying glass from the desk and raised it close to his face. It was a photograph of his father.

"Your very existence? I don't understand," Alex said.

"Your father saved us from being destroyed . . . by another magician!" Jack explained.

The King paced the floor. "Ah yes! That was long ago. His name was Vidok. We had been in his guardianship for quite some time. He was an outstanding magician. Performing illusions for royalty and presidents alike. But when his fame reached proportions he could never have imagined, he changed."

"He changed alright!" Jack said, twirling his finger next to his head.

"Thankfully, your father showed up and saw what he was about to do!" the Queen said.

"What was he about to do?" Alex asked.

"We were about to be barbequed!" Joker snapped. "I personally had the worst sunburn—"

"What about my father?"

"He was just eleven at the time," the King said. "He came to every single performance Vidok gave. And Vidok took notice. He adored your dad. So much so that he invited him backstage after every show. He shared many tricks with your father. His card maneuvers, levitations, and transformations were all secrets he had kept to himself until then. And your father learned them well."

"He certainly did," the Queen said. "He was a natural. Every time Vidok shared another trick with him, your father would show up to his next engagement having perfected it."

"But then something strange happened," King Anton frowned. "Vidok wasn't himself when he came back from an extended tour in Europe. And when your father came to see him after such a long separation, Vidok refused. He just sat in his chair after every performance with a vacant look in his eye. He was lost." The King shook his head sadly. "Then, on the very last day Vidok was to perform, your father returned, hoping Vidok would change his mind. That's when he heard our screams."

"Most people can't hear us, you know," the Queen nodded.

"That's right," Jack said. "All they see is an ordinary deck of cards."

"But not your father. He heard us, loud and clear!" the King continued. "He raced to the back of the building by the stage door where he found Vidok, half laughing, half crying. He had set a fire in one of the garbage cans. Each time the flames shot up he chose another cherished stage prop and dropped it in!" The King's hands moved as if he were polishing the air. "They were all laid out. His cape, his wands—"

Alex's eyes grew wide. "But, why?"

"Madness is a strange thing, son. It can creep into your soul like a venomous snake—seething, coiling—just waiting for the perfect moment to strike."

"One could say he just snapped!" the Queen said.

"So, so sudden," the King said.

Jack folded his arms. "You think you know someone, and then they behave so bizarrely."

Joker stood there staring at the three of them in disbelief. "Excuse me! The man was about to serve us up with a side of fries!"

The suits began to mumble as the King leaned close and raised his brow. "Just as Vidok was about to drop us into the flame, your father drove into him like a bull and shoved him against the wall."

"I don't know where he found the strength, but that little boy pushed Vidok clear to the ground!" the Queen said.

"That's when your dad grabbed us and ran," Jack said.

"He never looked back," the King said.

"What happened to Vidok?" Alex asked.

King Anton stroked his beard. "That was the day Vidok went completely mad. He performed his last trick off a bridge late that night."

"It was in all the papers. Sad really. Vidok would have loved that kind of press," the Queen said.

The King stepped aside. He raised his arm toward the Diamond, Spade, and Club families gathered behind him. "I speak for all of us when I say that day will forever be remembered as both the worst and greatest." He turned to Alex. "We've been with your father ever since. That is . . . until now," he added softly.

Alex stared at the King's pocket watch. He had spent endless hours by his father's side, mirroring his card tricks and maneuvers while his father worked out the details of his newest illusion. He had no recollection of ever seeing the curious deck that stood before him.

"I wonder why my father never introduced us."

"Actually, we did meet, but you were just a baby at the time," the Queen said. "I remember it as if it were yesterday. You were all of two when your father sat you down on top of this very desk." She shook her head. "He was attempting, unsuccessfully I might add, to stop you from crying while he struggled through a rather complicated trick we were working on."

The King chuckled. "That was a trick in itself!"

"That's right!" Jack said. "Mom, you started to play peek-a-boo with Alex, right?"

A warm smile grew on the Queen's face. "And that was the moment your father knew—"

"Knew? Knew what?" Alex asked.

"You played peek-a-boo right back!" the King chimed in. "Your father was beside himself watching the two of you interact. In fact, he was elated. You see, no one but your father and Vidok could hear our voices or see us moving about."

"Well, except for Snowball," Jack added. "Rabbits, dogs, birds—they can see and hear us, too!"

"You knew Snowball?" Alex's eyes grew wide. "Wow, he had the longest ears! I used to play with him when I was little. When he wasn't working with Dad, that is."

"Ugh!" Joker rolled his eyes. "That was one weird rabbit! He made me so nervous the way he freaked about everything. First, he had stage fright, and then he was claustrophobic. Then came the body issues. He drove me crazy with his questions, 'Do my ears look too big in this hat? Does my tail sag?'" Joker smoothed the creases in his jacket. "I told him straight out, 'Snowball, you had better get your act together or you're gonna find yourself on the end of some keychain!'"

The King squinted at Joker for a long moment then turned back to Alex. "You know, Alexander, more than anything your father wanted us all to be together. In fact, just recently, he thought you were ready to meet us now that you're older." The King dropped his head. "We were all so excited."

Alex bit his lip. He didn't want to cry, but he could feel his tears welling up. As he gently handed the watch to the King, his thoughts flew back to the day his father left him—forever.

Death by Magic

Alex ran down to the kitchen that morning and grabbed a bowl of cereal. Anxious to see the sketches for his father's newest illusion, he pushed his chair beside him.

His father took a sip of coffee, then boldly swept his pencil across the paper. "So today's the big day! Are you nervous about the game?"

"I wasn't," Alex said. He shoved a spoonful of cereal in his mouth. "But everyone keeps asking me, so now I am."

His mom slid into the chair across from them and cradled her mug. "Can you please swallow before you speak?"

"You're both coming, right?" Alex asked.

"Are you kidding? We wouldn't miss this for the world!" his dad said. "As a matter of fact, I'm leaving the aquarium extra early." He turned to Alex's mom and waved his pencil in the air. "We don't want to miss a single play."

"Absolutely!" His mom pointed to the corner of Alex's mouth. "This is going to be a super exciting game." She handed him a napkin and looked in the direction of the staircase. "That reminds me, I have to find my camera."

Alex waited for her to disappear up the stairs before wiping his mouth with his sleeve. He took another spoonful and peered over his father's shoulder. The page was filled with sketches of a giant whale from various perspectives. Alex's eyes jumped to the notations around the drawings. There were diagrams and fulcrums on one side, and a series of equations and measurements on the other. Scribbled along the top of the page in capital letters: *The Vanishing Orca*. Alex choked. "Dad, are you really going to make a whale disappear in front of an audience?"

His father raised an eyebrow. "Well, that's the plan. If I do, it will forever change the experience of sensory perception as we know it!"

Alex got goose bumps whenever his father spoke like that. It made him feel like anything and everything were possible.

Without saying a word, his father began another drawing on the back side of the paper. Alex watched a man in a wet suit emerge with flippers and an oxygen tank on his back.

"Wait! You're actually going *into* the tank with the whale? That is so awesome! Can I come? Please?"

"I'll tell you what. Once I have the specifics in place, you can join me, okay?"

Alex threw his arms around his dad. He plopped back in his chair, took another bite of cereal, and quietly studied the concentrated look on his father's face. A million questions flooded his brain. But he only asked one. "How do you create? I mean, how do you make all of this come together?"

His father placed his pencil on the table. It was as if this was the very question he had waited for Alex to ask. "Ah, the creative process—one of the great mysteries of the universe. Sometimes it can take weeks, or even years, before a trick takes shape. And then there are times when one just pops into your head, as if it were always there, waiting for you like an old friend. Now that's the sign of a serious magician!"

Alex dropped his chin in his hands. "I'll never be able to create a magic trick off the top of my head."

His father leaned close. "We magicians never say 'never.' That's a strong word, don't you think?"

"I suppose. But where do you even start?"

"Anywhere and everywhere. In school. In the car. Even when you're sleeping." His father glanced around. "Sometimes ideas come when you're just sitting in the kitchen." He reached for the saltshaker beside the bowl of sugar cubes. "Then, you start to build it, from the inside out." He placed the shaker in front of him.

Alex watched his dad pluck sugar cubes from the bowl. One at a time, he stacked them like tiny bricks around the saltshaker until it was completely concealed. "Patience," his dad said. That, my dear boy, is the secret to all great magic!" His eyes locked on Alex. He snapped his fingers, reached into the fort of sugar cubes, and lifted out a peppershaker!

Alex leapt to his feet. He leaned over and looked inside. The saltshaker was gone. From the corner of his eye, he noticed it sitting on the stove, way over on the other side of the kitchen.

"Wait. . . . How?" Alex raced over and picked it up. When he turned back to the table, the wall of sugar his father had built had vanished.

"What's that in your pocket?" His father wiggled his index finger.

Alex slowly reached inside. He gasped when he felt the sugar cubes crumble between his fingers. His heart racing, he rushed to the drawer beside the refrigerator and pulled out a deck of cards.

"Please, Dad. Please show me that dance trick before you go."

"I'm sorry buddy," his father said, gathering his sketches. "Today is not the day. We'll need more than a few hours of uninterrupted time, and I'm up to my ears."

Alex lowered his head.

"How about this?" He rubbed Alex's hair into a mop. "Let's get through all of today's activities, and we'll work on The Dance of Suits over the weekend."

Alex searched his father's warm brown eyes. Everything he ever hoped to be was smiling back at him. "You promise?"

His father grabbed a sugar cube and popped it into his mouth. He pulled his shoulders back and raised his hand. "I promise!"

Passing clouds offered little relief from the blazing afternoon sun. Alex felt drops of sweat trickle down his face from under his helmet as he scanned the packed bleachers. The score was tied, only thirty seconds left to the game and still no sign of his parents.

"You've got this!" Alex's buddy Tyler shouted from the defensive line. Best friends since first grade, he and Tyler had been practicing nonstop in the days leading up to this moment. Alex's team was on a winning streak, but all that could change in a heartbeat. This one was for the championship. There was no room for error.

A silence hung in the air as Alex readied for the faceoff. Crouched across from his archrivals, the Whitestone Eagles, he waited for the referee to resume the game. The whistle blew. Alex squinted through the blinding sun and plunged his stick forward, clamping down on the ball before his opponent. With seconds left, he sprinted across the field in a fast break. The fans cheered him on as he dodged the defensemen. They each tried to block him, but Alex, in one fluid motion, rolled to the left and then to the right. Darting behind his teammate, the only obstacle left between him and winning the game was the goalie. Quick on his feet, Alex wound up and aimed high, but at the last second, he ripped the shot low. It flew like a laser, right past the goalie and straight into the net.

The crowd went wild, stomping their feet and chanting his name, "Alex! Alex! Alex!"

Alex couldn't believe it. He had just scored the winning goal! He threw his arms up and danced in a circle. His teammates rushed over, hoisted him off his feet, and paraded him around the field. That's when he noticed the car. From high above their shoulders, he was pretty certain he only spotted one person— the driver.

The car turned the corner and pulled up to the curb. Even from that distance, once the door opened and his mom got out, Alex could tell something was wrong. He jumped down, threw his helmet to the ground, and ran across the field, pushing his way past the crowd of cheering fans.

"Mom, what's the matter?" His heart began to pound.

She grabbed him by the shoulders, her eyes red and swollen with tears.

"What is it? What's wrong?"

"Your father,"—her voice quivered—"he had an accident."

Alex pulled away. "Is he okay?"

She hesitated.

Alex held his breath.

"The oxygen tank. There was some kind of malfunction." She shut her eyes and tried to swallow. "They said it made this crazy hissing noise that agitated the whale. It started thrashing. It just kept thrashing! Alex, they couldn't control it. Your father was swimming too close. It knocked him unconscious. They couldn't get to him." She pulled Alex close. "He was so excited. This project meant everything to him. It was all he ever talked about." Her fingers dug into his arms.

Alex jumped away. The crowd roared and danced across the field while he stood there staring into his mother's eyes, numbed by her words.

It wasn't long after the funeral before Alex's mom realized the loan they had taken on their home to finance her husband's ultimate illusion made it impossible for them to afford to live there any longer. Even though Alex begged her not to, she decided it was in their best interest to move. Not just around the corner or a few miles away, but back to her childhood home in Orchard, Maine. There, she could get a job writing for the local paper. There, she could afford to buy a smaller place.

The day they moved, Alex could barely breathe. He somberly walked through the empty rooms for the last time. Happier moments flooded his memory. Just about every magic trick he had ever learned happened by his father's side next to the fireplace in his office. The long hallway that stretched from the front door to the kitchen was the perfect spot for sliding in cotton socks. Flashes of backyard barbeques, lacrosse practices on the front lawn, and Christmas morning surprises wrapped and waiting under the tree in the living room all swarmed through Alex's mind as he pulled the door closed behind him.

The house slowly vanished from sight when he and his mom drove away for the last time.

The sad past faded. Alex tried to focus on the fifty-three tiny people gathered in front of him on his bedroom floor.

"He left you a letter," the King said.

"A letter? From my father?"

The King nodded. "It should be in the desk."

Alex jumped to his feet. He pulled the top drawer open and plunged his hand deep inside. Nothing! He closed the drawer and opened the second one. Running his fingers along the top, he came upon a piece of paper jammed between the slats of wood. He wiggled it free.

The crumpled letter was folded in thirds. Alex sat on the floor and opened it. A small pen drawing of a top hat and wand adorned the right hand corner. It was written by hand. Alex knew the writing well.

My Dearest Boy,

I have often imagined what this day would be like for you. Is it Indian summer? Or is the ground covered in a blanket of snow? I know how much you enjoy the change in seasons. I also know if you are reading this, it is because I am no longer there with you.

Alex, you have made me proud more ways than I can count. For a man to have a son like you is rare. You have a remarkable gift. I have known this since you were a baby. Although I tried to guide you as best I could and help you nurture it, I know in my heart there is so much more for you to learn. That is why I am leaving you this extraordinary deck of cards. Take great care of them and they will do the same for you.

Remember, Alexander, you have a gift. Only you can hear these cards and see them come to life. No other person will have this ability. Even so, you must be extremely cautious with them, because these cards hold magic for whoever uses them.

My dearest friends Anton, the King of Hearts, and his lovely wife, Queen Olivia, will guide you. Take pleasure in their company, trust your instincts, and grow with them. Keep the magic alive, Alex. In time, you will be a better magician than I ever was.

I will love you forever,

Dad

P.S. Joker's bark is worse than his bite.

Alex read the letter again and again. Each time brought him closer to one certainty: nothing would ever be the same. His eyes filled with tears.

"Alexander Finn," the King said.

Alex wiped his face with his pajama top.

"Alexander Finn," he repeated, as the rest of the suits moved closer. "It is an honor."

Alex looked at the tiny faces smiling up at him. As difficult as it was to take it all in, by some inexplicable way, he knew his father was there too. He folded the letter and placed it on his lap.

"My father's wish was for us to be together," he whispered.

King Anton, Queen Olivia, and the fifty-one little people behind them all nodded.

"Then, you will always be with me."

He stretched his arm onto the floor beside the King and Queen. One by one, they all marched into Alex's hand, and with a snap, they turned into cards once again.

A Fruitful Start

"C'mon. Move it!" a man shouted outside Alex's bedroom window.

Alex stirred awake and stretched. Slivers of morning light shot through the shutters onto the wall of boxes. That's when the commotion began. At first, it sounded like an odd clip-clop. Then came a thunderous rumble. Suddenly the house shook and sent the top box crashing to the floor.

"Whoa! Go left! Go left!" the man screamed.

Alex kicked his blanket away to a cacophony of car horns and screeching brakes along the street. He leapt out of bed and pulled the shutters back to the strangest sight. Four horses were hauling a cart the size of a semi-truck down Walden Avenue. He winced when the men guiding it nearly sent it careening into a tree trunk. Then again, when it barely missed the row of cars parked along the block.

"Oh good, you're up!" his mom said from his doorway.

Alex pushed his face against the window as the cart continued down the street. "What's going on out there?"

His mom leaned over the desk beside him. "Boy, they're not wasting any time, are they?"

He looked at her quizzically. "Who?"

"The handlers of the apple float. Didn't I tell you about the Orchard parade?"

Alex cringed. As if moving to Orchard wasn't bad enough. "Parade? You're kidding, right?"

"Oh please, it's not that bad! But, from what I understand, there were some serious issues last year."

"Like what?"

"Well, they lost control of the float. Apparently, the horses took off, ran across several lawns, and destroyed a number of cars. Apples went flying everywhere. One of them hit the Mayor's wife in the eye! Poor woman was wearing an eye patch for weeks."

Alex's face lit up imagining the town covered in lumpy chunks of applesauce. "That's awesome!"

His mom gave him a nudge. She pulled her memo pad from her back pocket and flipped through the pages. "Here, this is from Mayor Davis himself. And I quote, 'Due to the unfortunate series of events during last year's Orchard Harvest Parade whereby hundreds of bushels of apples—three hundred and seventy-five to be exact—were thrown from the float when the horses got spooked, we are taking extra precautions this year. To ensure we do not have a repeat performance, we will be conducting trial runs along Walden Avenue so that we can get the horses used to the route.'" She proudly snapped her pad shut.

Alex's mom had just gotten freelance work as a reporter for the *Orchard Courier*. At first, Alex was happy for her, watching her dash out the door to a last-minute meeting with the Mayor. But as he glanced at the men grappling to control the cart and horses, he couldn't help feeling a little embarrassed for her. She would never have written an article like this in New York. But then a corny event like this would never have taken place there!

"Soooo, this goes on every year?"

His mom stumbled over the box filled with books that had fallen to the floor. "Only the consecutive ones," she grunted as she leaned over to pick a few up. "You know honey, we could have this place organized in—"

Alex interrupted, "I've got it, Mom! I'll take . . ." Just then, he noticed King Anton and Queen Olivia. They were strolling along the edge of the desk watching the scene outside unfold. The King turned to his wife.

"This is quite lovely, isn't it? I wonder what kind of coronation is taking place?"

In a panic, Alex slid in front of the desk to block his mother's view. "Don't you have an early appointment?" he shouted, attempting to drown out their voices. "Traffic is getting pretty bad out there!"

Busy arranging the books on his shelf, his mom paused, and looked at him curiously. "I'm quite aware that it's ten to eight, and YES I have to leave—eventually. Another meeting at the mayor's office," she mumbled, stepping back over to the window to check on the chaos outside.

Alex's heart jumped when Joker sailed beside him.

"Coronation?" He smirked as one of the horses unloaded a steamy trail of poop. "More like fertilization if you ask me!"

ECCHHH ACCHHH! Alex choked.

"Alex. Calm down. It's okay!" the King shouted.

"Are you alright?" his mother asked.

ECCHHH ACCHHH ACCHH. Alex kept slapping his chest, hoping to distract her from the activity behind him. "I think so!" he shouted. "Probably swallowed a bug or something!"

His mom patted him on the back. "Honey, I'm right here. You don't have to yell."

He coughed and threw his elbows up, attempting to move her away from the desk. But she quickly reached behind him and grabbed the King, Queen, and Joker.

"Here, put these cards with the rest of your deck before you lose them."

"My what?"

"Your cards. Where do they belong?" she said.

The King, Queen, and Joker stood smiling in the palm of her hand.

"I tried to tell you son, she can't see us the way you do . . . remember?" the King said.

"Ohhhh, right." Alex laughed in relief. "I forgot how this works."

"You forgot how what works?" his mom asked.

Alex slipped the cards from her hand, hoping to appear at ease. "No . . . I mean, YES. I forgot to put them back with the rest." He awkwardly stepped backward and dropped them in the drawer.

His mom turned to leave but paused in the doorway. "You sure you're okay?"

"Me?" He shrugged. "Yeah, Mom, totally. I'm all good."

"Alright then. I have to run. I left breakfast on the table for you. Just promise me you'll be out of here by eight-thirty. You don't want to miss the bus again."

"Don't worry, Mom, I've—"

"Yes, I know, you've got it!" she said. "Just don't be late."

Alex wasn't at all concerned, but just so his mom couldn't say he didn't try, he went through the motions anyway. He got dressed, ate his cereal, and grabbed his backpack. He locked the front door, but when he reached the corner, he realized he'd left his cards behind. He ran back inside, dashed up the stairs, and took them from the drawer. Suddenly aware he had ninety seconds to make the bus, he flew down the stairs and slammed the door behind him. He raced across Walden, then down the hill to Bay Avenue, but the bus had just turned the corner. Alex stood there in the lingering fumes and watched it disappear in the haze.

WIGGLE ROOM

It was, at most, a forty-minute walk along the main road to the steps of the schoolhouse. But Alex, curious to see beyond the limits of Orchard, decided on a different route that morning. He wound his way through the backstreets of ivy-covered stone walls and red clapboard cottages. He walked by the docks where fishermen dressed in rubbery yellow overalls unloaded their lobster traps. He climbed the steps of the narrow railroad overpass and waited for the trains to rush beneath him. Standing there, the wind whipping through his hair high above the ochre and crimson treetops, he imagined he was soaring—back to Ridge Park, back to his friends, back to the life he knew.

It was painfully quiet by the time he reached the thick glass doors of Orchard Middle School. The scent of floor wax and coffee mingled in the air as he raced through the empty corridor to the gymnasium. Slipping into his new school's gym T-shirt and shorts, he studied the yellowed photographs of former football coaches that lined the wall above the lockers. Alex's heart sank. How could his mom send him to a school that knew nothing about lacrosse? More than ever, he missed his teammates, and the only sport he really loved. In the distance, a whistle blew. He quickly placed his cards in his pocket and disappeared through the doors to the field outside.

Mr. Schnitzer, his new gym teacher, tossed a football from one hand to the other while he spoke to the class. Alex ducked behind the widest kid and dropped to one knee, pretending to tie his sneaker.

"Mr. Finn, is that you way back there?"

The tone of his voice made Alex cringe. He got to his feet and stepped out from his hiding place. "Good morning Mr. Sch—"

"Late again, huh!" Mr. Schnitzer yelled—his thundering voice only to be outdone by the piercing shrill of his whistle.

Alex stood there mortified as his classmates covered their ears with their hands and glared in his direction. A tiny snap later, things went from bad to worse.

"You have GOT to be kidding!" Joker shoved his sleeping mask aside and stomped out of Alex's pocket.

"Uhh. Not now!" Alex whispered.

"Not now?" Mr. Schnitzer repeated.

"No, no! I meant—"

"Whoa!" Joker trotted underneath his T-shirt and shimmied down the back of his shorts. "Quite the uniform! What? They didn't have plaid?"

"Joker, get back here this instant!" the King shouted from Alex's pocket.

The class laughed as Alex awkwardly wiggled and jerked his shoulders and hips.

"I'll get him!" Jack shouted

"STOP!" Alex twitched.

Mr. Schnitzer raised an eyebrow and leaned closer. "What did you say?"

Alex's mouth opened and closed like a guppy. His eyes inched up the front of Mr. Schnitzer's sweatshirt until he was forced to tilt his head way back. He lifted his right foot, then his left, and started running in place. "I . . . just . . . don't . . . want . . . to . . . STOP!"

Mr. Schnitzer's eyes tightened as the class burst into fits of laughter. He raised his whistle and sent another deafening blast into the crevices of Alex's brain. Everything went silent.

"Well then, Mr. Finn. I suggest you start running!"

"Running? But I thought we were playing foot—"

"RUN!" Mr. Schnitzer commanded, pointing to the track behind him.

Alex's face felt red hot. He stepped onto the track and watched his classmates snicker at him as they divided into teams.

"I hate this place," he murmured.

When class finally ended, Alex hung back in the locker room and waited for the last boy to grab his backpack and leave. Once the door shut, he heard a familiar *SNAP!*

King Anton appeared and leaned against his open locker. "If I may offer my deepest apologies, Alexander. At times, Joker has proven himself to be a force of nature."

Alex yanked his T-shirt over his head. "Well, maybe you can convince him that this place is bad enough without his help."

The King nodded. "I know this has been tough on you. Maybe in time, this will all just fade into one bad memory." He stepped closer. "Everything will turn around, you'll see. As your father would say, things aren't always what they seem."

"Did he bring you to school with him?"

"All the time. We were inseparable."

Alex balled up his gym socks and threw them in the locker. "I wonder what his gym teacher was like."

The King grabbed onto his crown and watched the sock ball fly over his head and land on Alex's gym shorts. He turned back to Alex. "Well, it was quite a while ago. Although, I do remember he blew his whistle at your father an awful lot, just like your Mr. Schnitzer."

Alex sat on the bench tugging his shoelaces into tight knots.

"So tell me, what is the rest of your day like?" the King asked.

Alex shrugged. He pulled his schedule from his backpack. "French, English, art, then lunch," he murmured.

"Très bien!" The King bowed. "We are but a pocket away if you should require our services." He jumped back into Alex's jacket but popped up again a second later. "Hey! Why can't a bike stand on its own?"

Alex shut his locker. "I don't know, why?"

"It's two tired!" The King offered a toothy grin.

Alex wasn't much in the mood for a laugh. He appreciated the King's words, but he knew in his heart they were just that. Nothing but words. Ever since his father had died, adults would grab him by the shoulders or pat his head and say things like, "Everything will be alright. It just takes time." Alex hoisted his backpack over his shoulder and headed out of the locker room. He was convinced that no one had a clue as to what he was really going through. And now, as if things weren't bad enough, Joker had made him look like a fool.

Mrs. Worthington was already conjugating the verb "to go" on the blackboard when Alex stepped into the room. He made his way across the creaky floor, hoping no one in his French class had witnessed the fiasco in the gym. He sat there for most of the period, slumped in his chair with his face buried in his book. The image of Mr. Schnitzer's flaring nostrils kept popping into his head.

By the time art class rolled around, Alex began to feel at ease. Mr. Queazel, a slightly gnomish looking man wearing a wrinkled shirt and rainbow-colored tie, surprised the class with a slide show on the cave drawings discovered in Lascaux, France. Alex was grateful for the anonymity the dark room provided, but as the slide show clicked through at a snail's pace, he found himself bored to tears. He tried to stay awake by drawing little cavemen wearing hard hats and using electric drills in his notebook. When Mr. Queazel discovered it, he made Alex rip out the page so he could pin it on the bulletin board for everyone to see.

Alex had had enough—first Mr. Schnitzer, now Mr. Queazel. The minute the lunch period bell rang, he grabbed his backpack and slipped out the back door. He hurried through the crowded hall with his head down, determined to get through the rest of the day without incident. But the afternoon was far from over.

LUNCHROOM FIASCO

"**W**as that you?" a stocky, blond boy asked.

Alex dropped his head and pretended not to hear. He had barely taken a bite of his cheese sandwich when someone elbowed him deep in his shoulder blade.

Alex shifted uncomfortably in his seat. "I'm not sure what you mean?"

The boy put his face so close that his nose nearly touched Alex's cheek. "Yeah, that was you!" He dropped his lunch tray on the table and wiggled his body as if he had ants in his pants.

Alex took a sip of his milk and swallowed hard. "What are you doing?"

"An imitation of you on the field this morning." The boy laughed as a rowdy group from gym class crammed in next to him. They looked like they were packing the bleachers at a football game.

Suddenly aware that the last table in the corner of the cafeteria might not have been the best location after all, Alex turned back to his sandwich. He took a bite and then another, hoping no one noticed his face was glowing like a hot coal.

"C'mon! Won't you dance for us?" the boy said, sending his buddies into a fit of laughter.

"Anyone sitting here?" another voice interrupted.

Alex looked up. A girl with brown, shoulder-length hair was standing across from him holding her lunch tray. She looked familiar, but before he had a chance to answer, she slid into the seat opposite him. Just then, a spitball came flying past his right ear. It jumped across the table and landed in her plate of French fries.

"That's not funny, Dylan!" She turned to Alex and rolled her eyes. "They're like crow magnums."

Several more spitballs flew overhead. "I think you mean Cro-Magnon," Alex said. "You look familiar."

"Yeah, I sit right behind you in Mr. Queazel's class." She grinned. "Cute drawings."

"Ha-ha." Alex smirked.

"No, seriously, those little cavemen? They were really funny!"

"Comin' right at ya, Lindsay," Dylan shouted. Suddenly a barrage of spitballs bounced around them like tiny hailstones.

"Why don't you get a life?" Lindsay said.

"Hey, Wiggles, what's your name again?" Dylan asked.

Alex felt Dylan's hot breath on the back of his neck. He was hoping this particular Cro-Magnon would rip into his lunch rather than continue ripping into him. No such luck.

"It's Alex."

"Well—Al—ex, seeing how Schnitzer's taken a liking to you and all, we sure hope you'll be trying out for the football team." Dylan snickered. "Maybe you can show us how to squirm!"

Alex sighed. He shook his head, thoroughly disgusted, while Dylan and his buddies continued to mimic him. He gulped down the last few bites of his sandwich and grabbed his backpack to leave before a wide-eyed boy at the other end of the table caught his attention. The boy was holding a deck of cards. He tried to shuffle them but quickly became frustrated when they slipped through his fingers.

Alex dodged the next round of spitballs and slid beside him, retrieving a few of his fallen cards from the floor.

"Thanks." The boy smiled.

Alex watched for a moment as the boy tapped the deck against the table and divided them. Once again, just as he began to shuffle, the cards collapsed in a heap.

Alex turned and faced the boy. "What's your name?"

"Shawn."

"Okay, Shawn, place your thumbs tighter against the top, like this." Alex separated the cards into two piles and shuffled them through his fingers. He shimmied them downward, then up again.

"Wow. That was so cool!" Shawn said.

Lindsay leaned across the table. "Know any tricks?"

"I was just gonna ask the exact same thing. See Lindsay?" Dylan said, jutting his chin out, his mouth filled with half eaten fries and ketchup. "Us crow magnums should stick together." All at once, the boys at his table began grunting like cavemen.

"Oh shut up!" Lindsay turned back to Alex. "Anyway, can you show us something?"

Alex hesitated. Part of him wanted to grab his backpack and leave, but then a few students at the other tables started gathering around.

"Can you do tricks?" one of them asked.

"Wow! Let's see!" another said.

Alex cradled the deck in his hands. "Yeah, I think I know one."

With that, he snapped his wrist and transformed the cards into a perfect fan. He snapped again and they disappeared.

"Whoa, that was awesome! Do another one!" Shawn said.

A few curious students from the opposite side of the cafeteria inched closer while Alex continued to entertain the crowd with a series of fans. Each one burst open in rapid succession. *Pop, pop, pop!*

Everyone whistled and applauded. Alex felt a rush of excitement he hadn't experienced in a long time. Thinking back on what the King had said in the locker room, he seriously doubted things would ever turn around. But there he was, glancing at the crowd, a look of wonder on their faces. He had to consider that maybe the King was right. Alex widened his stance and held the deck before him. "Okay, one last trick." He bent the cards back and sprung them high above his head in an arch. His schoolmates gasped as they shot from one hand to the other like fluttering birds. That's when one of Dylan's spitballs blasted through the air and hit Alex on the cheek. Alex stood there, his face stinging, while the cards spiraled to the floor.

Someone let out a giggle, then another. In a matter of seconds, the entire lunchroom erupted. Dylan shoved his way in front of Alex and began his wiggle dance for the crowd. He shimmied his hips and threw his hands in the air while the crowd roared with laughter. Alex stepped aside, his hands empty and his mouth hanging open.

"How do you have the time to eat with all this commotion?" Mrs. Logan marched over and glared at the unruly group before her. "Dylan, take a seat!"

Alex collected the cards from the floor and handed them back to Shawn. Furious at himself for not leaving when he had wanted to, he grabbed his backpack, slipped through the crowd, and waited by the cafeteria entrance for the bell to ring. *Just three more classes,* he told himself as he marched off to math on the second floor.

"Wait!"

Alex turned. It was Mrs. Logan making her way up the steps behind him.

"I'm glad I caught you. You ran out of there so fast. I have something here that you may be interested in." Her silver bracelets jangled as she rifled through her briefcase. "I'm on the entertainment committee for the grand opening of the Orchard Commons Mall." She handed him a flier printed in a bubbly font with purple and yellow starbursts.

Calling all Kid Magicians . . . Ten years and older.
Help us celebrate the opening of Orchard's newest mall,
where you'll find a little magic in every store!

Alex couldn't understand what Mrs. Logan was thinking. Hadn't she just seen what happened? He shook his head and handed it back to her. "I'm not interested."

Mrs. Logan followed him up the stairs. "Alex, I am terribly sorry."

He turned as a flurry of students rushed by. "For what?"

"For the way those boys treated you just now. It was uncalled for. It's hard to understand the mind of a seventh grader, I have to admit. Sometimes they can be very mean!"

"Tell me about it."

A few more kids squeezed through when he yanked the second-floor door open.

"I think it's very impressive that you do magic tricks," Mrs. Logan said.

"Yeah, well, a lot of good it does me."

"Personally, I think you should be very proud. Your father was the Incredible Finn, no?"

Alex let go of the door handle. He looked Mrs. Logan in the eye. "My father was one of the best."

"I know. Your father often performed in Warwick. That's my hometown." She smiled. "For the longest time, before I became a drama teacher, I wanted to be a magician."

The second bell rang through the empty stairwell.

She handed the flier back to Alex. "Well, just think about it. It would be wonderful to have you there."

Alex stood by the entrance of the second floor and watched Mrs. Logan disappear up the stairs. He reread the flier then shoved it into his jacket pocket.

By three o'clock, it seemed to Alex that most of the school had seen or heard about the wiggly dance Dylan had concocted. The minute the last-period bell rang, he sprang from his seat, grabbed his backpack, and raced down the front steps into the thickening mist. He was halfway to his school bus when he spotted Dylan leaning against its open doors. Alex's shoulders sank. He wanted to get home, but there was no way he was going to spend another second fending off Dylan's taunts. He slipped back into the fog and waited for the bus to leave without him.

CALLING ALL MAGICIANS

Alex took extra-large steps, pushing through the soggy air with his head buried under his hood. He charged past a row of shops, managing to crash into more than a few of the official Orchard Parade flags planted along the sidewalk, as if he needed another reminder of the town's corny obsession with its upcoming festivities. Those ridiculous flags were popping up everywhere—the front steps of the bank, by the entrance of the Maritime Museum, outside the ice cream parlor. He couldn't help but pause when he saw the sign boasting, of all things, lobster praline ice cream!

"Gross," he mumbled.

Finally, he reached his front door. Rain trickled down the back of his neck as he stood there digging through his pockets in search of his key. The family across the street had just come home. A mother, a father, and two young boys hurried inside laughing as they brushed the rain from their hair. Alex slammed his backpack on the porch and knelt down beside it.

Joker leapt from Alex's pocket with the key in hand. "Looking for this?" He landed on the floor, jumped on the key, and surfed from one end of the porch to the other.

Alex wiped the rain from his eyes. "Yes Joker, I *am* looking for that!" He chased Joker from one side of the porch to the other. Each time, Joker slipped between his legs, then his hands, then his legs again. Finally, Alex made a quick thrust forward, cornering Joker with his foot. He wrenched the key out from under him.

"Well!" Joker huffed. "I was only having a little fun."

"You've had quite a bit of fun today, haven't you?" Alex jiggled the key in the door. "Thanks to you, I'm that new kid who does the wiggle dance!" His waterlogged sneakers squished as he clomped down the hallway into the kitchen. He yanked the dish towel off the stove and turned to a yellow sticky note stuck to a bowl of apples. Alex read it while he dried the back of his neck.

Honey,

I came home around 2, but just got another call for a last-minute interview. If I'm not home by 7, there's sliced cheese in the fridge. Make yourself a sandwich, and try one of these amazing apples! I'll be home as soon as I can.

Love You,

Mom

"Perfect!" Alex grumbled, staring at the pile of Orchard's finest crop arranged in front of him. Yet another reminder of his horrible new life in this horrible place they moved to. He grabbed a couple of pretzels instead, marched up the stairs to his room, and emptied his pockets on the desk.

King Anton appeared, shaking the rain from his robe. "Not exactly the best of days, huh?"

Alex threw his jacket in one corner, his backpack in the other, then plopped down on his bed. "I hate this place!" he said, attempting to unknot his soaked shoelaces.

"I can see that," King Anton said.

Alex kicked his sneakers under the bed then slid into his chair by the desk. He sat there tapping his fingers, silently fuming.

The King moved closer. "Perhaps—"

"The thing is—it's not just Dylan or Mr. Schnitzer, or the even the school." Alex slammed his fist on the desk. "It's this whole town! All anyone cares about is that stupid parade." He leaned closer to the King. "They don't even have a Chinese restaurant! I still don't understand why we moved here!"

The King cleared his throat. "You know, Al—"

"It's not *my* business to tell you what to do." Joker interrupted. "If it were me? I'd just walk right into that school like I owned it!" With his chest out, he held little Emilio like a baton and marched across the desk, up Alex's stack of schoolbooks, and down the other side.

Alex slapped his hands against his face, rolled his eyes to the ceiling, and let out a moan.

The King sidled up to Alex. "What if—"

SNAP! Queen Olivia and Jack appeared from the deck.

"Shhh! That is not helpful, Joker," the Queen whispered. "And by the way, it is extremely impolite to eavesdrop. This is a private conversation!"

The King scratched his beard, "You might—"

"Don't you have somewhere you need to be?" Jack chimed in. "Some Joker convention or such?"

Joker threw his nose in the air and turned toward the rest of the cards piled beside him. "Really!" he hissed.

The King stomped his foot. "Might—I—have—a—word?"

Everyone went silent. The King gave a nod, at which point, the Queen, Jack and Joker disappeared to the opposite side of the desk. He turned to Alex. "What if—"

"I just don't get it," Alex interrupted. "Am I really supposed to unpack all my belongings and pretend everything is okay? It's not!" He shot up and accidentally thwacked his hand against one of the boxes. "I hate this, this Orchard—ville—town or whatever it's called!" He sank in his chair, rubbing his throbbing hand. His eyes fell on the photograph of his father. He leaned close, touched the glass, and dropped his head on the desk.

The King took a long deep breath. "I can certainly understand how you feel, Alexander. It's not easy starting over, is it?" He settled on the edge of Alex's science book and let out a chuckle. "You know, you kind of remind me of your father when he was your age. I'll never forget the day he came home from school, fit to be tied!"

Alex raised his head. "Fit to be tied? What does that mean?"

"It's sort of . . . it's a figure of speech. It means he was so angry he could burst," the King said. "So, to continue my story, your father was rushing home to get ready for his first magic show when he slammed his thumb in the door. It got so swollen he couldn't do any card tricks. He was so mad at himself that he kicked his books to one end of his room and his shoes to the other."

Alex let out a laugh.

"But that sore thumb didn't stop him." The King wagged his finger. "He not only went to that six-year-old's birthday party with his thumb wrapped like a mummy, he wrapped the other one, too. He named them Coco and Willie and put on a puppet show for those kids."

The King stepped in front of the frame and studied the photograph. "Your father was quite clever. Always coming up with solutions when everyone else was scratching their heads in search of one. Talented and remarkably courageous."

Alex listened. He tried to imagine his father at eleven years old putting on a puppet show.

"He was a lot like you." The King smiled.

"Really?" Alex grinned.

"Yes, really!"

"Yeah,"—Alex shook his head—"but I'm not courageous. Sometimes I don't know who I am anymore."

The King stepped closer. "Well, maybe you've never been in a situation where you had to be courageous."

Alex looked up. "You mean like when my dad saved you?"

"Exactly. Your dad didn't see himself as courageous back then. He didn't even know what that meant. Was he terrified? Yes! But he didn't let that get in the way. He just reacted to our cries for help without thinking of the consequences. That's courage. You don't wear it like a sweater. It just comes."

Alex wondered if what the King said was true. *Does it just come?* These days he didn't feel particularly courageous or confident about anything. Then again, if it were true, how would he handle a situation like that?

Then he remembered the flier Mrs. Logan gave him. He reached for his jacket, pulled out the wadded piece of paper, and smoothed it out on his desk. "There's this contest."

The King pulled his reading glasses from his vest and set them on the tip of his nose. "Calling all magicians. When is it?"

Alex raised his brow. "This Saturday."

"Well that's great, Alex! See. That's courageous! And you know what? It might be a wonderful opportunity for Orchard, Maine to meet the real Alexander Finn."

"The *real* Alexander Finn . . ." Alex murmured. He couldn't help imagining how proud his father would have been to see him perform with their special friends. "Do you really think we can do this? It's only a few days away."

"I don't see why not," the King said. "Perhaps it would be prudent to get everyone together for a little practice." He turned to the deck, and with a snap of his fingers, the rest of the suits materialized. "Alexander has an announcement to make," he said in his most commanding voice.

At once, the Diamonds, Spades, and Clubs gathered beside King Anton, Queen Olivia, Jack, and the rest of the Heart clan.

"If this is about reorganizing Alex's room," Joker said, gliding forward. "I would like to take this opportunity to offer my services. A nominal fee, really. Shillings are preferred. However, I also accept—"

"I'm thinking about entering a magic contest," Alex jumped in.

The group mumbled excitedly.

Queen Olivia clasped her hands together. "Oh! How wonderful, Alex!"

Jack shook out his legs and cracked his neck. "Wow! It's been a while since we've worked, but I think I can get in shape in a few weeks."

"But, but we don't have a few weeks," Alex stuttered.

Everyone froze as Jack moved closer. "Well uh, what do we have?"

Alex hesitated. "The contest is this Saturday."

Jack's face went pale. He leaned over and rested his hands on his knees, as if he was catching his breath.

"With Alexander's permission," the King interrupted, "it's always best to start fresh. I suggest we all begin our practice sessions first thing tomorrow!"

With that, he snapped his fingers, sending the rest of the suits back into a pile on the desk.

"Jack doesn't look too happy," Alex said.

The King stroked his beard as if he were petting a cat. "Jack is—well, he tends to freeze if he feels he's under pressure. It's all in his head. He just has to work through it. He'll be fine." He put his tiny hand on Alex's. "You know we're always here for you—right?"

Alex leaned close. "Yeah."

"Hey!" The King grinned. "What does a magician like to keep up his sleeve?"

Alex chuckled. "I don't know. What?"

"His arm!"

Alex wrinkled his face. As corny as his jokes were, he had to admit, he got a kick out of the King's silly nature. He placed the cards in their lacquered box, tucked them in the drawer, and pulled out a pad of paper. He made a list of all the tricks he could think of. There were fans and flourishes and cards that float. There were shuffles and cuts and sleights of hand. All he knew. All he understood. Except for one.

Calling
Magicia
Tricks
Out of This World ✓
Triumph ✓
Floating Card ✓
Ambitious Card ✓
Color Change ✓
Three Card Monte ✓
Royal Ace ✓
Dance of Suits
? ? ?

A Major Disaster

"Four days?" Jack snapped, shoving the cover off the box. He climbed out and began to pace from one end of the drawer to the other.

The King followed behind Jack. "What makes you think we can't work out a routine in four days? Why, we've pulled off magic shows with the Incredible Finn in half that time!"

Jack spun around and faced his father. "Yes, but that was after years of practice. By then, all it took was a look from him, and I knew exactly what to do next." He leaned his head against the side of the drawer. "That kind of relationship takes time."

The Queen appeared, her gown falling over the edge of the box. "But you have all the skills. It's really just a matter of putting the pieces of the puzzle together."

"It's not that. I mean—it's more than that. You know what happens to me!"

"Son, in all the time we were with the Incredible Finn, that only happened once," the King said. He scratched his beard and thought for a moment. "Okay, maybe twice, if we count that other trick you couldn't—"

"You've made your point Anton," the Queen said.

"And I don't want it to happen again!" Jack snapped. "With all that practice, I still couldn't make that spin. The Dance of Suits was ruined because of me!"

In truth, it had been a major disaster. The theatre was packed. With every seat taken, just as many spectators were wedged shoulder to shoulder in the rear of the auditorium. The room went dark. Seconds later the Incredible Finn stood center stage in a brilliant circle of light. A low hum washed over the audience as he placed his cards on the floor beside his feet. Jack was on top of the pile. Hopeful and excited, he waited for his moment.

The Incredible Finn stepped slowly stage left. He gave the signal—a snap of his fingers. Jack took a deep breath and closed his eyes. His card rose. The deck followed close behind, spinning and twirling, mounting and diving. The audience jumped in their seats, their eyes glued as the cards undulated upstage then down along the apron's edge. Back and forth, they whipped like the tail of an anxious animal until Jack slipped out of sync. He twisted to the left, caught himself, and twisted again. The impact was immediate. Cards crashed one into the other. They fluttered across the stage in all directions while the audience howled with laughter.

Jack leaned against the desk drawer and lowered his head. "That was a horrible moment. Not just for me—for all of us! Sometimes I still wake up in the middle of the night and see Alex's father's expression—the look of disappointment on his face. And the audience. I thought they'd never stop laughing." Jack looked his parents in the eye. "It's no wonder he never used us to perform The Dance of Suits. That was all my fault, and the worst part is I can't go back and fix it!" He folded his arms. "All I can do is avoid taking that kind of chance again."

"Jack honey," the Queen said. "Life is all about taking chances. Sometimes we have to fail a few times before we get it right.

What if the Wright Brothers avoided challenges? Or Thomas Edison? Or Marie Curie? This world wouldn't be the same without their dedication and passion. If they were the least bit afraid to experiment, we'd all still be wandering around in the dark ages!" She laughed. "How will you ever know what you're capable of if you don't at least jump in and try? My advice? Try not to be so hard on yourself."

The King nodded in agreement. "And if I recall, the Incredible Finn wasn't even supposed to perform that night. He was asked to replace another magician who came down with the flu. Son, we all did our best under the circumstances."

The Queen stepped over and stroked Jack's golden locks. "I think you're spending good energy worrying about nothing. Let's save it for practice and see how far we get?"

"I suppose." Jack sighed. "Still . . . only four days?"

"Your mother is right," the King said. "Sounds to me like you're talking yourself into a problem." He pulled out his pocket watch and grinned. "A lot can happen in ninety-six hours."

Jack sat down and rested his head in his hands. "A lot, indeed!"

THE PRACTICE SESSION

With his newly compiled list of magic tricks as his guide, Alex prepared over the next few days just as he'd seen his father do. Each morning, before school, he propped his mirror against his wall. First, he worked on his sleight of hand maneuvers. Studying his reflection, he tucked the cards deep in his palm and slipped them under his wrist, concealing them up his sleeve. He repeated the exercise over and over, assessing his technique in the mirror until his moves were seamless. After school, he'd rush home to practice the more complicated shuffles and fans. Each session ended with an exercise. He'd crack his knuckles and then weave the cards under and over his fingers. By Thursday, his movements had become so smooth the cards glided effortlessly in his hands.

"Excellent job!" Alex announced. Just as he placed the cards on the desk, Joker jumped to his feet.

"Well hallelujah! You've had us work on every trick under the sun these last few days." Joker turned to the rest of the deck. "I don't know about you, but I'm quite sure I'm ready for that contest."

Alex rubbed his hands together. "Well actually, there is one last trick . . . The Dance of—"

"Ohhhhh, I don't think so," Jack groaned. "Anything . . . I repeat, anything, but that. I HATE that trick! I'm just no good at it. Please Alex, can't we do The Sybil? It's so easy. I can do it with my eyes closed. Hey! What about The Four Burglars? That's a fun one. You get to tell a story, and we get to hide."

Behind Jack, the other suits quietly waved their hands in a panic. It was clear they didn't want to take part in another fiasco with Jack. Alex fell back in his chair, disgusted. His eyes drifted to his father's photograph and the proud expression on his face after he had successfully performed The Dance for the first time. Alex remembered the late nights when he'd sneak down to his father's study to watch him practice this elusive trick. How exciting it was to catch a glimpse of his dad's arm sweeping through the air or the back of his head jerking and bobbing as if he were conducting an orchestra. His focus was unlike anything Alex had ever seen. Even the way his body moved was as if he possessed some inexplicable energy. Alex was convinced there was something much more tangible to this trick. Something that he didn't possess.

When his father finally performed The Dance of Suits in front of hundreds and hundreds of fans, Alex had a first-row seat. Dizzy with excitement, he watched the Incredible Finn do the impossible. Floating the cards above him, he sent them waltzing in pairs across the stage. They twirled and dipped and bobbed as the orchestra played from the pit below.

From that day on, Alex was relentless, pleading with his father to show him how he made the cards dance. But a trick of that caliber required time, and his father's hectic schedule only complicated matters. That last morning they spent together, his father had promised. Finally, Alex would learn the secret.

"Look, I'm not planning on performing The Dance of Suits tomorrow," Alex explained. "I just . . . I need to know it." He grasped the photo of his father. "I just have to."

Jack folded his arms. "Your father only attempted it with us once."

Alex shook his head, hopeful.

"Right away, he saw 1 had a problem," Jack went on.

"1 believe the word he used was klutz!" Joker rolled his eyes. He turned to Alex and explained, "You do know your father chose a plain old, dog-eared, tired deck of cards for his big performance . . . can you imagine?"

The suits mumbled loudly.

"Oh please!" Joker threw his hands in the air. "I'm just telling the truth!"

Jack moved closer to Alex. "Look, I don't want you to get your hopes up."

Alex nodded.

"Alright." Jack sighed. He gestured to the rest of the suits to join him and climbed on top of the pile. "If it's that important to you. But I'm warning you now, this isn't going to be pretty."

Before Jack had a chance to reconsider, Alex grabbed the deck. He shut his eyes and tried to recall every detail he could. But, much in the way he remembered his dreams, he only saw fragments.

The first step he was sure of. Alex spread the cards along the edge of the desk and slowly raised his arms. He wiggled his fingers as if he was playing an invisible piano. At once, the cards began to quiver and rise. Fascinated as they hovered above the desk, he froze for a second, then moved his hands crazily up and down in front of his face. The cards became a tangled frenzy and toppled to the floor. He rushed over, picked them up and tried again. This time he moved his arms in a circular motion, and the cards turned upright. They began to spin slowly when Jack made a weird humming noise.

"Watch out!" several tiny voices rang out.

Jack's card skidded straight into the King of Clubs, who crashed into the Four of Diamonds, who collided with the Ace of Spades. The jumbled mess of cards spun to the ground at the same moment Jack flipped wildly across the room and disappeared.

From the heap on the floor, Queen Olivia jumped up and scanned the room, "Goodness, Jack. Where are you?"

A sheepish voice called out, "I'm over here!"

One by one, the rest of the suits got to their feet. They tidied their ruffles and robes while Jack crawled out from behind the bed and hobbled back. "I keep telling you, but no one seems to be listening, I'm never going to be any good at this trick!"

Alex couldn't help but smile. Remembering his father's favorite expression, he got on his knees, leaned close to Jack, and whispered. "We magicians never say 'never.' That's a strong word, don't you think?"

Jack gave him a long look. "Yeah, I guess so."

"Listen son, Alex is right." The King stepped over and gave Jack a pat on the back. "Try to stay positive. If you focus and keep practicing, eventually you'll get it right!" He glanced around the room for a moment and then pointed to the window by the desk. "Try focusing on an object right in front of you, like that window."

Jack followed his father's outstretched arm across the room.

"When you spin, keep looking at it, like this." The King pulled his shoulders back and slowly began to turn. With each rotation, he looked directly at the window. "See? Now you try it. I'll bet with a little more practice you'll be orbiting in place and not around the room."

Jack studied the window for a moment. He planted his feet firmly, straightened his back, and raised his elbows. Just as he was about to launch into a spin, there was a tap on the door.

Alex's mom poked her head inside. "Hey there."

Alex shot around, startled. Then he remembered that she couldn't see the tiny people in front of him. All she could see was a deck of cards scattered by his feet.

"My editor just called. He and his wife want to take us to their favorite Friday-night spot."

Alex looked at her puzzled. "There's a night spot in Orchard?"

She leaned against the door and laughed. "I guess it's all relative, right?"

"Italian?" Alex asked.

"It's a pretty popular place," she sang.

"Do I have to go?"

"You love Italian food. I thought you'd be all excited!"

"It's just not the same," he murmured.

His mom sat on the edge of his bed and picked his jacket up from the floor. "I know this is a big adjustment. It is for me too." She suddenly looked far away.

Alex got off his knees and sat by his desk. Together they stared at the unpacked boxes.

"You know what I miss?" she said.

Alex turned to her. "Everything?"

"The dumplings at Hong Kong Garden."

Alex chuckled. "Yeah, those were good."

"Really good!"

"Then why can't we go home?"

She got up and stepped by the window. "Alex, this is our home."

Alex sank in his chair.

"Look, I know it seems like a different world up here. If you just give it half a chance, it's really not that bad. Sure, it's got its share of hokey traditions. What small town doesn't? It's also grown quite a bit, I'm happy to say." She turned to him, adding, "There's a lot going on here!"

He ran his finger over his cards. "Like what?"

"Well, there's the Orchard parade next week and that new mall opening tomorrow." She gazed out the window. "Wow! I can't believe we'll finally have a mall. When I was a little girl, we had to drive all the way to Bangor to find a halfway decent department store! Boy, I wish I could make it tomorrow. I've got this—"

"Let me guess. You have a deadline." He sighed.

"Yes. And the more freelance work I get, the more money we can save to fix up this place." She rubbed the top of his head. "You should definitely check it out. Maybe you can find us a good Chinese restaurant!"

Alex didn't tell her he already knew about the mall. That in fact, he was planning to take part in their magic contest. Knowing she couldn't be there because of her job, he didn't feel all that bad keeping it his little secret.

From the corner of his eye, he noticed the flier on the desk. He slid over and stood in front of it.

"Promise me you'll try," his mom said.

Alex slipped the flier in the drawer. "Try what?"

"To give Orchard a chance?"

He took a deep breath, held it for a second, then slowly released the air.

She kissed him on the forehead. "We should get going."

Alex waited for her to leave before he spread his cards on the bed. "I'm really sorry," he explained. "I was hoping we could get through The Dance at least once."

"Not a problem," Jack said. He folded his arms behind his head and propped his feet against the edge of his card. "It is totally, perfectly fine with me if we have to postpone!"

"What's important is that you and your mom had a chance to talk," the King added. "What did you think about her suggestion?"

"I told her I'd try to keep an open mind," Alex said.

Queen Olivia beamed. "That's all a mother could wish for."

"And don't worry for a second." The King shook his finger. "We have all the time in the world to practice The Dance of Suits. It will happen."

"Yeah," Alex agreed. He gathered the cards and tucked them in his pocket. "We do have plenty of time, don't we?"

Joker popped his head out. "If you ask me, you folks are just asking for trouble, plain and simple!"

JUST AN ILLUSION

Mrs. Logan tapped the microphone with her finger. "Welcome to Orchard Commons, where you'll find a little magic in every store!" She was standing on the stage in the center of the mall, checking the sound and lights in anticipation of the magic tournament.

Alex's eyes grew wide as he stood by the entrance. High above Mrs. Logan, rays of sunlight poured through the glass atrium onto clusters of colorful balloons and large billowy banners. As he wove his way through the crowd, it suddenly dawned on him that this event was a much bigger deal than he'd thought.

By the time he arrived backstage, Mrs. Logan had disappeared. He poked around where twenty or so contestants were gathered. Each one was dressed in a different costume. Mothers and fathers, brothers, sisters and grandparents all hugged and posed for photographs beside them.

Alex's heart sank. *Maybe I should have told Mom about this.*

"I hate to be the bearer of bad news." Joker jumped from Alex's pocket. "But there is no possible way we can win this. Just look at those getups!" He turned to his little scepter Emilio. "These things are always fixed, you know. Somebody knows somebody, and before you know it . . ."

Alex glanced down at his T-shirt and jeans. The whole thing suddenly felt wrong. He definitely should have told his Mom. Maybe she would have made him a cape or helped him locate one of his father's wands tucked in the boxes in the attic. Throngs of people rushed by him, but Alex felt lonelier than ever. He turned and ran back toward the entrance, shoving past the crowd so quickly he almost lost his balance.

"Hey Alex, it's great to see you!" Mrs. Logan grabbed him by the shoulders and nudged him toward the stage where the other contestants had congregated. They jostled through the crowd, but as they got closer, Alex's feet fixed to the floor. "Come!" she said. "We're about to start!"

Alex wanted to say he was sorry and that he just couldn't go through with it. He wanted to tell her that the other contestants seemed better prepared, and he didn't want to make a fool of himself again. Then he remembered how determined his father had been pulling off that injured-thumb puppet show. Alex couldn't help but wonder if he would have done the same. Mrs. Logan stood there waiting. He took a deep breath and followed her the rest of the way.

Mrs. Logan introduced the first two contestants, identical twins, Brian and Davy. They both had a mouthful of glistening braces and sported top hats over their curly brown hair. The only way to tell them apart was Brian wore a red bow tie and Davy wore a yellow one. The boys walked around and asked for the audience's help. Alex studied them as they moved about mirroring each other's trick.

They knelt beside two women in the front row and spoke in unison. "Pick a card!" Each boy held out a pen. "Please sign your card, show the audience, and put it back in the deck." Both ladies followed the instructions. The twins circled the stage, occasionally bumping into to each other while they shuffled their cards in synchronized motion. Davy paused in front of the woman who had put her card in Brian's deck. Brian paused in front of the woman who had put her card in Davy's deck. Davy pulled Brian's card from his deck. And Brian pulled Davy's card from his deck.

"Yes! That's my card!" one of the women shouted. She stared at Davy and the card in his hand. She pointed to Brian. "But I put my card in *his* deck."

"And that's my card!" the other woman said. She snatched her card from Brian, pointed to Davy, and held it high. "And I put *this* card in *his* deck."

"How'd they do that?" a young girl shouted.

Alex smiled to himself. *Clever move switching bow ties rather than the cards!*

One by one, the next few contestants stepped onto the stage to perform. Wallace, a rather pale twelve-year-old dressed in Goth, made the crowd wince with his *needle through the arm* illusion. Reilly, a thirteen-year-old with unusually large, round glasses appeared to mentally twist a table full of silverware. P.J., a lanky eleven-year-old with copper-colored hair, juggled everything from books to eggs, after which, the maintenance crew was called to mop up the stage. As Alex watched the men scoop up bits of cracked eggshells, his thoughts drifted back to the first magic trick his father taught him.

His father wrapped his large hands around Alex's. "The magic is within you," he said softly. He pushed Alex's thumbs into the side of the deck and bent the cards back until they slowly began to shuffle through his tiny fingers. "There will be many challenges in your life," he warned. Alex sat on the floor and watched him tap the cards with his knuckles then fan them into a circle. "And some will take you off course." At once, the cards jumped up and turned into chattering teeth. They chomped through the air in every direction then fizzled away. "Remember Alex, if you keep steady and stay focused, the magic will come."

His father's words faded when a woman shouted in Alex's ear.

"That's my little girl, Dee-Dee!"

Alex glanced at the woman. He followed her finger toward the stage where a ten-year-old wearing a wide-brimmed hat had just grabbed the microphone right out of Mrs. Logan's hand. Dressed in her black and white cowgirl outfit and matching boots, the girl waved a quarter at the crowd and began singing a country tune. She snapped her fingers and the silvery coin disappeared. She trilled through most of the second verse, then suddenly lunged forward and grabbed the coin from the ear of a man standing to the side of the stage. Dee-Dee cocked her head and smiled coyly at the crowd.

At first, Alex was impressed with the young girl's dexterity. She didn't look that obvious when she slipped the quarter out from under her thumb before plucking it from the man's ear.

Dee-Dee's mother tapped Alex on the shoulder. "Hey there, I'm Mrs. Fardull." She reached out her hand. "You must be new to the neighborhood."

Alex turned to her. "How did you know?"

"Honey, I know everyone in this town." She laughed.

"Oh, uh, I'm Alex, by the way." He shook her hand. "Nice to meet you."

"My Dee-Dee is in all the talent shows and pageants." Mrs. Fardull batted her eyes and adjusted her hair. "Just like I was when I was her age."

Alex tried to act interested in Mrs. Fardull's rambling while Dee-Dee pranced across the stage. But then she tripped and her disappearing coins jumped from her pockets and rolled across the floor like tiny wagon wheels. She ended her song with her arms outstretched and halfway stuck in a split.

Mrs. Logan rushed onstage and hoisted her up by her armpits. "Thank you, Dee-Dee." She grabbed the microphone and looked in Alex's direction. "And now, I'd like to introduce our last contestant, Alexander Finn!"

Not one to shy away from performing, Alex turned to walk up the stairs and onto the stage when he was overcome by the oddest feeling. Like a huge brick had dropped in his stomach. He actually heard his insides squirming when he stepped in front of the audience. He swallowed hard, barely able to make eye contact with the crowd that clapped and whistled before him. But that wasn't the worst part. Once the heat from the floodlights hit him, beads of sweat dripped down his forehead. He wiped his face with the palm of his hand and began to shuffle his cards, but they stuck to his fingers!

"Hey, Houdini! What's taking so long?" someone shouted.

A low mumble rolled through the crowd. Alex shaded his eyes with his clammy hand and peered through the blinding lights. A few spectators shook their heads. Others whispered and giggled. His attention jumped to the back row. It was Dylan! He stood up, along with his buddies from the football team. They cupped their hands by their mouths and shouted in unison, "Hey, Houdini! Whatcha got up your sleeve?" One by one, they began the wiggle dance.

This was Alex's worst nightmare, with one exception. It wasn't a dream.

THE VANISHING ACT

Alex stood there in a panic. He wiped his hands on his T-shirt as laughter flooded the mall. It echoed down the corridor of shops and kiosks then bounced back even louder. For a second, he felt strangely outside himself, as if he were watching the whole thing from the ceiling. Soon, he was back on stage under the blazing lights when he heard a tiny voice.

"Alex!" King Anton shouted.

Alex shook his head, in an attempt to clear the daze.

"You can do this!"

Alex kept blinking. He tried to focus on the King, who was leaning from his card and waving his arms to get his attention.

"You can do it!" the King repeated.

Alex stared into the King's eyes until a peculiar calm took hold of him. The laughter that surrounded him suddenly gave way to the sound of the banners billowing above him like sails on a ship.

Mrs. Logan was about to jump back onto the stage when Alex stepped forward. Determined to put his fears aside, he took a deep breath, flicked his wrists and launched into a series of fans. Not a sound could be heard except for those of the cards gliding through his fingers. In rapid succession, they flew and snapped and spun at Alex's command. One after the other, they popped open like bursting fireworks and then just as quickly, disappeared. The cards moved so fast it was as if his fingers had a mind of their own.

The crowd leaned forward when he stepped across the stage holding the three of clubs for all to see. At first, they seemed confused, looking at one another, shrugging as if they were waiting for something to happen. But once they realized the card he was holding had transformed into the ace of spades, the audience began to buzz with excitement and curiosity. Alex marched across the stage again, and this time the ace of spades transformed into the king of diamonds. The audience was still in the middle of a collective gasp when he plucked the four deuces from the deck. He leaned over to hand them to a woman in the first row. She turned to the crowd and raised her arms high. Alex waved his hand above her and snapped his fingers. When she looked back at the cards, they were no longer twos but all queens.

By the time he began his final trick, the mall was humming with anticipation. Alex spread his cards and gave the King a subtle nod before he flicked him from the deck. The King jumped up. He flipped twice and slipped back into Alex's hand.

Next, Alex plucked Queen Olivia's card from the pile. She launched into a somersault then dove headfirst back into place. Finally, he flicked Jack's card. Jack twirled like a top. He spun above Alex's head until, quite suddenly, he lost his balance and spiraled out of control toward the audience. His face filled with fear as he moved farther away from Alex's grip. The crowd jumped back as the card flashed toward them. Alex shot forward. He leapt up and grabbed Jack as if he were catching a bird in flight. Poised with his hand in the air, he landed on his feet by the edge of the stage with a smile on his face. The entire mall erupted into cheers and whistles. No one realized what had happened.

Alex took a deep breath. He turned to leave the stage just as Mrs. Logan dashed over, grinning from ear to ear. She grabbed the microphone off its stand and guided Alex beside the row of contestants standing in position on the side of the stage.

"We want to thank all the talented young people that performed today. Weren't they all marvelous!" She applauded, encouraging the audience to join in. Mrs. Logan extended her arm to the five adults seated at a table draped in a black skirt. "We'd also like to thank the wonderful judges, the hardworking business owners of Orchard. Let's give them all a hand for their time and generous support."

Alex gazed at the row of judges. He hadn't even noticed them tucked in the corner. There were three men and two women, each making notes on their clipboards. His eyes jumped to the table beside them where several trophies were lined up. One in particular caught his attention. Floating above a polished black marble base, two hands encased in glass performed a card trick. From where Alex stood, it looked like a hologram. When he shifted his head, it changed tricks! He couldn't take his eyes off it.

One of the male judges stepped over and handed Mrs. Logan three envelopes. For a moment, she held them to her heart, smiling at the young contestants that stood before her. It was obvious she was proud of all of them.

"Okay!" she said, tearing the first envelope open. "Our second runner up is, Reilly Simmons!"

The audience clapped as Reilly marched over to accept her trophy. She shook hands with the judges and Mrs. Logan then moved back into the line. Alex leaned forward to get a glimpse of the contestants. They all looked so excited in their sparkly costumes that glimmered under the lights. Some had their fingers crossed. Others were waving anxiously at family members.

Joker is right. There is no way we can win, Alex thought.

Mrs. Logan ripped the second envelope. "Our first runner ups are . . . Davy and Brian Lucas!"

The crowd applauded as the twins stepped over. They tipped their top hats, accepted their trophies, and stepped back in the line.

Mrs. Logan held up the last envelope. Alex's head began to pound. His heart beat so loudly it felt as if it was banging on his brain. She ripped the envelope open and leaned close to the microphone. Alex inched closer too. He squinted hard as she moved her lips. Still, he couldn't make out a word.

Wait? What did she just say?

Everything went into a kind of silent slow motion. Mrs. Logan tucked the envelope under her arm. She turned in Alex's direction and began to clap. The contestants turned and clapped, and the audience followed. Alex glanced at his cards. The King and Queen were clapping and pointing excitedly behind him.

Alex spun around. The most exquisite trophy he had ever seen was coming right at him. With a huge grin plastered on his face, he took it in his arms and held it tight. Alexander Finn stood before the residents of Orchard, a proud winner. All at once, the pounding in his head faded and the sound of applause filled his heart.

Seconds later, the other contestants crowded around him. In a way, it seemed strange. Just a few moments earlier, he was being heckled. Now he was surrounded by well-wishers who patted him on the back and shook his hand. Alex answered all kinds of questions about his array of tricks, but as soon as he could slip away, he moved to a quiet part of the stage and fanned his cards across the table.

"We did it!" Alex smiled.

The cards quickly transformed and rushed toward him.

"That was some save!" Jack said.

The Queen clapped. "Well, you were remarkable!"

"Just fabulous!" Joker added.

A look of pride filled the King's face as he stepped closer. "Undoubtedly, this is a very special moment for us all!"

"A very special moment," Alex whispered.

There was so much more to say. Alex wanted them to know everything that was in his heart at that moment. How much the King and Queen's encouragement meant. How badly he felt for Jack, and how he looked forward to working with him. How Joker could make him laugh and want to pull his hair out in the same breath. But most importantly, he wanted them to know how utterly grateful he was to his father for leaving him this special family. Alex gazed at his dearest friends. He struggled to find the words—the right words—when suddenly he was besieged by fans.

"How did you make those cards fly?" a father holding his wide-eyed little girl asked.

"It's magic!" Alex winked.

Another boy held out a pen and paper. "You were great!"

Alex was taken aback. "You—you want my autograph?"

The boy nodded excitedly. "Someday, I want to be a magician just like you!"

Those words caught Alex off guard. It wasn't that long ago he'd announced the same thing to his father. He smiled at the boy, stepped away from the table and reached for his pen. Alexander Finn began signing his name on whatever was placed in front of him.

A girl admired her newly autographed T-shirt. "This is so cool!"

"You were totally amazing!" A mother smiled, her little boy peaking from behind her.

"Hey there," another voice called out.

Alex looked up. It was Lindsay from his new school.

"Well, this went a whole lot better than the lunchroom!" she kidded.

Alex's tongue grew thick. "Yeah, I guess."

"You deserved to win." She pulled off her baseball cap and handed it to Alex. "Those tricks were way cool!"

He looked at her skeptically. "You really want my autograph?"

"Are you kidding me? I don't know how you got those cards to do what they did, but when you're a famous magician, this hat may be worth something!"

Alex waited a moment for the crowd to die down. "They're magic, you know," he whispered.

"Yeah, right!" She laughed.

Alex looked around again. "I'm serious. My Dad left them for me. They're very unusual cards."

"Okay, if you say so." Lindsay swatted him with her cap. "Just sign it!"

"Oh look!" Queen Olivia whispered. "How wonderful for Alex. He's making new friends! You know, for a while I was getting worried."

"Why?" the King questioned. "Everything works out over time. You just have to have patience!"

"He is the man!" Jack shouted.

"Look at our Alex." Joker clapped. "I knew he would win. And just like that, he's an overnight sensation!"

The King, Queen, and Jack shook their heads as Joker prattled on. It seemed the more he babbled, the more dramatic he became. He scurried back and forth across the table in search of a handkerchief to dab his crocodile tears. Suddenly, a hand with thick stubby fingers, sporting a sapphire pinky ring, cast a shadow over the deck. The hand hovered for a moment, then snatched the cards from the table.

A SMALL OVERSIGHT

"Seriously, where did you learn to do tricks like that?" Lindsay asked. "They were really awesome!"

Alex sat across from her at the food court watching the crowd disperse into the mall. He looked at his hands, still in shock that he had actually won. "My dad was a pretty incredible magician." He shrugged. "I guess I got the bug from him."

"I'm surprised the Orchard Parade zombies didn't get hold of you!" Lindsay scanned the food court as if they were lingering nearby. "They're always on the lookout for fresh blood."

Alex stared at her. "What is it with them?" He chuckled, totally relieved she wasn't one of them. "They are like so weird! Have you walked around this neighborhood lately? They've taken over with their bumper stickers and street banners. This stuff would never go on in Ridge Park." He turned to her quickly. "No offense."

"None taken," she said. "I grew up here, but sometimes I even cringe." She jumped up, placed her hand on her hip and pretended to hold a big juicy apple. "An apple a day . . ."

"Is the Orchard way!" they sang in unison.

She turned to Alex's trophy, studied the hologram inside, and tilted her head from side to side. "Wow! Check this out! It's so cool!" Suddenly, she stopped and stared at him. "Wait! How do you have time to practice, with all the homework Mr. Burroughs gives out? Seriously, it's like his whole purpose is to fill our lives with mold experiments."

"Well, it's not easy, but I have to confess—"Alex leaned close—"I actually practice when I'm doing my homework."

"Really?" She grinned. "You mean your *magic cards* won't do your homework for you?"

"Very funny. Yep. I always have my cards nearby." He felt around in his right pants pocket, then his left. Nothing. "I usually keep them in my . . ." He dug through his jacket, pushed himself away from the table, and spun around.

"My cards! WHERE ARE MY CARDS?"

Lindsay glanced around her. "That's strange. Where could they have gone?"

"I don't know!" He dropped to his knees and looked under the table.

"Well, they must be around here somewhere," she said, staring back toward the atrium.

They searched everywhere. Under the stage, behind partitions, inside the potted palms. They even searched the garbage containers that ran the length of the mall.

Alex flung trash in every direction. "This can't be happening. What am I going to do? I have to find them!"

Lindsay turned to him, puzzled. "Can't you just get another deck of cards?"

"NO!" Alex fired back.

Her face dropped.

"I'm sorry," he said, running his hand through his hair. "Look, I know you don't believe me, but they really are special cards. They were my father's. He left them to me and now—now they're gone!"

Lindsay patted his shoulder. "Maybe they'll show up."

Alex had a sinking feeling deep inside. He stepped back on the stage and walked in circles, not saying a word. From the corner of his eye, he spotted something shiny. It looked like a sequin glimmering on the floor. He stepped closer and slowly dropped to his knees. It was the King's gold pocket watch. He picked it up and clicked it open, revealing the tiny photograph of his father. Alex shut his eyes. The reality of the situation was becoming all too clear. . . .

His dearest friends were gone!

POKER FACES

The cards hit the green felt with a thud. Swirls of smoke churned above, coiling like a snake into a blinding light. Two men leaned close.

"Well, well, what have we here!" said the larger man with the wavy red hair.

"Mr. Raymond, check this out!" The man wearing the sapphire pinky ring spread the deck across the poker table. "You should have seen this kid perform at the mall. He was doing some crazy things with these cards. Like they were"—his eyes turned wild with excitement—"supernatural!" He picked them up and shuffled them a few times. "Call me crazy, but I'm telling you, something's up with these cards. How else could a three of clubs turn into an ace of spades right in front of you?"

Mr. Raymond folded his arms. "Uh-huh."

"Okay, I know what you're thinking. It must be a mirage or something. But get this. Right after the contest, I caught that kid hiding in the corner. And you know what he was doing?"

Mr. Raymond let out a sigh. "I haven't the foggiest."

Theo pounded his index finger on the poker table. "He was talking to these cards like they were his best buddies!"

"And I suppose they talked back?"

"Well, I didn't actually hear them, but I did overhear him talking to some girl. He told her they had magical powers!" Theo held up a few of the cards and shook them. "I'm telling

82

you. Something is up with this deck! Watch this." He leaned in until his nose almost touched the King. "Uh. Huh—hullo, little cards. This is Theo. Can you maybe do a little shuffle for me?"

Suddenly, the cards shifted around on the table.

Theo cocked his head and smirked. "See! I told you!"

Mr. Raymond stared at the deck. His eyes narrowed and turned to Theo. "Are you pulling my leg?"

Theo laughed. "Don't believe me? You try it!"

Mr. Raymond paused for a moment. He braced his hands on the edge of the table and leaned close. "Hello, little cards. Can you jump for me?"

At once, the cards hopped up in his face. Mr. Raymond jerked back. He circled the poker table, his eyes focused on the deck. "Remarkable!"

Theo grinned and pulled the two of clubs from the pile. He sat down at the poker table and carefully placed it in front of him. "I have a better idea. Okay little card, would you mind turning into the ace of spades for me?" The two of clubs quivered for a second, then it magically morphed into the ace of spades. Theo banged his fist on the table. "What did I tell you!"

"Outstanding," Mr. Raymond murmured.

"That's what I'm saying! Can you imagine what kind of a scam we could pull off in a couple of poker games?"

"High stakes poker games!" Mr. Raymond said, easing back in his chair. "I can think of a number of people I'd like to take to the cleaners—if you know what I mean."

Theo plucked Joker from the deck and strolled to the window. "Yeah, I was kind of thinking the same thing."

"Finally," Joker gushed. "Someone who truly appreciates my effervescence!"

"What are you doing?" Mr. Raymond asked.

"I'm . . . uh"—Theo hurled Joker out the window—"just getting rid of that Joker. Bad luck and all. We've had enough of that lately, haven't we?"

"Oh no they didn't!" Joker shouted as he spiraled through the air. He twirled like a leaf, gently swaying from side to side until he crashed into a stack of wooden crates and tumbled to the ground.

King Anton, Queen Olivia, and Jack watched in horror from the poker table as Joker disappeared into the night.

Mr. Raymond puffed on his cigar. "Why don't we give these magic cards a try? Maybe if we treat them real nice, they'll win us some magic moola!"

"Magic moola." Theo snickered. "That's a good one! And, if they don't win us magic moola? What then?"

Mr. Raymond coughed up an evil laugh and nodded toward the window. "I can assure you, my friend, their fate will be a whole lot worse than that Joker card!"

With a quick snap, the Diamonds, Spades, and Clubs all huddled behind the Heart family. King Anton, Queen Olivia, and Jack stood front and center with their arms locked.

"Where are we?" the Queen whispered.

"My dear, I'm afraid we've fallen into some rather devious hands," the King said.

"What's going to happen to us? Jack stuttered.

"And where is Alex?" they all cried out.

Joker stood there in the dank alleyway, glaring up at metal bars that ran across the window, when something scurried behind him. "Ewww. What was that?"

He held Emilio to his chest, but before he could get to his feet, the wind lifted him like a kite. It pulled him into a tight circle that spun between the buildings and every garbage can and dumpster in its path. Joker tried to reach for the handrails by the cellar, but the wind sucked him deeper into a wild tangle of debris. It twisted and turned through the alleyway until finally, it spat him out into the middle of the street. He landed on the road seconds before a car raced by and ran over him.

Joker lay there incensed. The very idea he could be considered so unimportant as to be thrown from a window! And now, his best silk jacket was covered in tire marks. Joker stared down the alleyway. He had no issue scaling that brick wall up to the windowsill and marching back inside. He'd tell them a thing or two! Maybe they wouldn't actually hear him, but when had that ever stopped him from speaking his mind?

Joker peeled himself off the road. With a snap of his filthy fingers, he jumped to his feet and began wiping the grease from his pants. That's when he noticed something curious. There, in the Cider Shoppe's window, stood a little man in bright green lederhosen. Flanked by jugs of apple cider stacked like pyramids, he held out a mug while his body twisted from side to side. Joker limped closer. He pushed his face against the glass and realized the little man was nothing more than a mechanical display.

Suddenly, light filled the end of the hallway. Joker dropped behind the toy man and watched the stocky shadow slip through a backroom door and creep through the corridor. As it skulked past the window, Joker could just make out the crooked slant of his nose. It was Theo!

Theo's eyes shifted from one side of the store to the other. He grabbed a jug of cider, rushed back through the corridor into the smoky poker room, and slammed the door.

Joker gazed out at the street. His thoughts turned from his own ordeal to Theo's words. Had he heard right? Were they really going to force his friends into cheating people? What exactly was going on in the back room of the Cider Shoppe? Joker needed to get help. Somehow, someway, he would have to find Alex—and fast!

HOCUS POCUS

Sickened by the loss of his cards, Alex didn't sleep at all that night. He paced from one end of his tiny room to the other, trying to figure out what had happened. He even went back to the mall on Sunday just to make sure he didn't miss anything. But when he pulled the heavy glass doors open, he froze. It was as if the magic contest had never taken place. The stage had been dismantled, and the balloons and banners were gone. All that remained the same was the afternoon light flickering overhead.

Alex roamed through the mall, trying to remember where he had been. He searched the row of food court vendors and checked the bathrooms. He poked his head in every store. For a split second, there was a glimmer of hope when he discovered Aunt Rose's Consignment Shop.

The window was filled with an eclectic mix of toys, decorative stained-glass lamps, and old cuckoo clocks. He rushed inside, hoping he might get lucky and find the cards there. Squeezing through the narrow aisles of scarred furniture and mothball-scented rugs, he discovered a corner piled with children's toys and dolls. Maybe Aunt Rose found his cards and added them to her collection. He got on his knees and poured through the old board games, bins of broken chess pieces, and tattered playing cards.

Alex was beginning to lose hope. He shuffled back through the shop entrance and paused in front of an ornately framed mirror. Standing there, staring at his distorted reflection in the warped glass, he couldn't help thinking what a disappointment he was turning into. How could he have been so careless as to lose his dearest friends, his father's most precious gift?

On the walk home, Alex wandered past the docks. He lingered for a while, watching the ferry churn across the harbor. *Should I tell Mom what's going on?* he wondered. *But what can I say? Dad left me a deck of talking cards, and I lost them? For sure, she'll think I've gone loopy from all the pressure we're under.* Alex was at a loss, but he knew it probably wasn't the smartest idea to bring his mom into the mess he'd made. He was already keeping way too many secrets from her as it was. He couldn't even keep his promise to meet the school bus on time. It was best to avoid her until he knew what to say.

Every time she knocked on his door, he'd grab a book and pretend he was studying. If she had to run to a last-minute meeting with the mayor's office, he'd make believe he was asleep when she returned. He'd lay there, tears welling up in his eyes, remembering the silly jokes the King shared or how encouraging the Queen could be. He thought about how much he looked forward to working with Jack, and how—in all his folly—he even missed Joker.

He thought about how much the cards had meant to his father. And how he placed his own life in jeopardy, charging forward and pushing Vidok to the ground to save them. Alex never knew anyone with that kind of courage. His dad was his hero. If only he'd had the chance to tell him so. Alex slid into his chair and reached for his photograph. He held it close. His

father's words echoed in his ears. "Never stop believing in the magic within you." He dropped his head and sobbed.

Monday morning, the corridors of Orchard Middle School were abuzz. Alexander Finn had won the magic tournament.

"Congratulations, Alex!" a group of girls sang out.

"Nice work!" another classmate shouted.

Alex kept walking. He looked straight ahead as if they were talking to someone behind him. Just as he opened his locker, Mrs. Logan caught up with him.

"Hey Alex, I'm glad I found you. I hope you don't mind, but I hung this up in your honor." She gave him a warm smile and pointed across the hallway.

Alex turned. On the wall behind him was a large poster with his photograph. He was holding his trophy and grinning from ear to ear.

Mrs. Logan pointed down the hall. "By the way, you left it at the mall. "It's in my—"

Alex slammed his locker door. "Left what?"

"Your trophy. I have it in my—"

"You can keep it!"

Furious that Mrs. Logan ever suggested the contest and frustrated by his own stupidity, Alex rushed off. All he could think about was finding his friends. In every class he went to, he'd slump into the corner seat and stare out the window. He prayed they were safe. He tried to imagine the face of the person who might have stolen them. Were they his age? Were they old? Was it one person or a group? He gazed onto a street full of strangers. Some rushed for the bus, some walked their dogs, and others window shopped. It dawned on him that the thief could be just about anyone.

At lunchtime, Alex hesitated by the entrance of the cafeteria. He watched Lindsay settle in at their usual table and glance around every so often. He couldn't bear to talk with her. He was afraid if he did, he might burst into tears. That's all Dylan and his "spitball squad" would need to see. Instead, he hid on the other side of the cafeteria. A couple of students gathered around him as he ate his sandwich. They held out their decks of cards, hoping he might show them a trick. He just shook his head and waved them away.

The days dragged on. Alex did everything in his power to keep his distance and avoid everyone in his path. Then Friday arrived. It had been nearly a week since the contest. He stopped by his locker to drop off his math book before his next class. That's when he discovered the poster. He hadn't realized how much work Mrs. Logan had put into it. "Congratulations Alexander Finn" was printed in large letters above a photograph of him holding his trophy and smiling ear to ear. But someone had drawn a mustache and beard on his face and scribbled the words "Hocus Pocus" over his name.

Alex stepped in front of it. He ran his fingers over the graffiti, remembering the incredible moment when his cards jumped for joy. He leaned his head against it, heartbroken by how everything that mattered in his life had vanished. Everything.

Just then, he heard giggling. Alex spun around. A group of girls hanging out by their lockers stared at him, each whispering to the other. Dylan slowly rose up from behind them.

"Hey, Houdini! Why don't you just make it disappear?"

Alex clenched his fists. He lunged forward and ripped the poster from the wall, glaring at the huddled group as he tore it into pieces. He turned away and shut his eyes. He had to get out. He had to find his friends.

Dylan and his posse's mocking taunts echoed behind him as Alex charged toward the stairway. He raced down the two flights and threw himself against the exit door. It burst open with such force that it slammed back, almost knocking him over. Alex stood there and drew in the crisp afternoon air. Finally, he was free.

"Well if it isn't Mr. Finn," a familiar voice rumbled. "Where might you be off to in such a hurry?" Mr. Schnitzer stepped out of nowhere, his gym whistle dangling inches from Alex's face.

Alex's heart was racing. He thought about making a run for it, but that would only make matters worse. He dropped his head and tried to catch his breath.

Mr. Schnitzer pulled the door open. "Shall we?"

Alex took a long look out at the street before he stepped back inside. His cards were out there somewhere. He just knew it.

JOKER'S WILD JOURNEY

Joker never noticed that the afternoon sky had turned gray, or that menacing clouds loomed above. He barely even flinched when lightning cracked around him. All he knew was he had to find Alex. He wandered the streets, stopping every few blocks in hopes of finding a familiar landmark, but there was nothing but old buildings and cobblestone streets to guide him. He held Emilio close. "I think we're lost!"

In a flash, a giant bolt of lightning exploded beside him. Joker was sent hurling through the air. He crashed face first into a brick wall and slid to the ground, landing beside a shoebox and a stack of newspapers left for garbage. He crawled inside the box and sat there in a daze, blinking stupidly. Pounding raindrops felt like boulders banging on his skull. With the little strength he had left, he dragged a section of the newspaper over to the box. Wet and shivering, Joker collapsed in the dark.

The next morning, a deafening piercing noise shook him awake.

"What on earth!" Joker grumbled grabbing his little scepter.

Suddenly, the shoebox jerked. He tried to sit up and rub his eyes, but his head slammed against the lid. He ran his fingers along the edge trying to push the cover away when he realized the soggy newspaper he had used for a blanket, had dried in the morning sun. Joker was entombed in paper–mâché!

"I am so not a piñata!" he said banging on the lid.

At once, the piercing noise turned to a gnashing, grinding growl. A moment later, the shoebox flipped over and Joker was thrown to the other side. Jammed in the corner, he kicked and clawed until he finally cracked a hole big enough to wedge his face and arm through. Joker couldn't believe his eyes!

Sailing above a mountain of rotting fruit and greasy containers, Joker and his shoebox were on a downward slide, straight into a garbage truck's compactor! Joker was frantic. He banged and punched, finally wiggling free at the exact same moment the steel rollers caught the edge of the box. He dove into the air and somersaulted onto the street just as the shoebox was crushed in a churning sea of rubbish.

There wasn't much time to soothe his frazzled nerves because as soon as the garbage truck turned the corner, the ground began to rumble. The sound grew louder, as if an earthquake had just rolled beneath his feet. But this wasn't an earthquake. It was a surge of rainwater rushing down the street. And it was heading straight for Joker!

"This is quite possibly the worst day of my life!" he screamed to Emilio as he turned to run.

He stormed ahead, glancing over his shoulder now and then. The raging flood drove forward like a tsunami, burying everything in its path. He quickened his pace, but he was no match for the force of nature mounting behind him. The wall of water rose and swelled. It grew so high that it blocked the sun. And then it happened. . . .

The thunderous wave came crashing down and swallowed him whole.

Joker whirled head over foot in a murky maze of bubbles and wash. It rolled and pounded him every which way until he became so disoriented he couldn't tell which way was up. But then, the tiniest slivers of sunlight broke through. Joker followed the light and shot to the surface like a rocket.

"I stand corrected." He choked between gasps of air. "This *is* the worst day of my life!"

He coughed and gagged, trying to catch his breath, but the current moved quickly. It dragged him through the street and swept him around the corner. Joker watched in horror as empty soda cans and broken tree branches sailed by and disappeared into the sewer! He raised his weary limbs and tried to swim back the way he came, but every stroke only brought him closer to a most unfortunate end.

"Oh, what a dreadful departure!" he cried.

All he could do was shut his eyes and hope it would be over quickly. He clutched Emilio to his chest and braced himself. But just as he was about to be pulled into an underworld sea of sludge, something sharp dug into his collar. His body lurched forward, then up. Joker hung there, dangling on the edge of the storm drain. Seconds later, hot puffs of fishy air wafted across his face, a stench so noxious it set the bells of his hat ringing.

"Well, here's a keeper." The mangy cat purred.

Joker dared not twitch. Stifling every instinct to shriek or carry on as he normally would, he shut his eyes and played possum. *It's quite possible,* he reasoned as the cat laid him on the pavement, *if I explain how my friends are in terrible trouble, kitty would understand and let me go.* But when he spied the scruffy feline pawing what appeared to be the remains of a mouse, its lifeless brown ears and matching pelt beside him, Joker felt faint.

He tried to slink away, but the cat circled, batting him every so often to see if there was any life in him. Joker's heart pounded.

His muscles stiffened as the cat's course tongue inched its way across his face like sandpaper. *My end is certain,* Joker thought as he held his breath.

"Eeeek!" a desperate squeak cried out from the raging flood.

"Eeeek!" the squeak moved closer.

The cat shot around. Its tail twitched from side to side before it bound for the curb, preparing to hook another poor unsuspecting victim.

Joker sat up. If there was any chance of escaping, it was surely that moment. He quietly got to his feet, careful not to step on any mouse parts, and slipped around the corner.

Joker ran as fast as his tired body would go. He limped across the park and over a bridge. He hobbled along a thick tree-lined path until he was certain he was safe. Shuffling along, he realized he had come to the end of a driveway.

"Well that's just perfect!" he panted.

He stood there, hands on his hips, glaring at the garage door when a curious shadow crept up behind him. Its slinky form moved slowly, deliberately. Joker held his breath and turned. It was the cat, its weight shifting from one paw to the other, ready to pounce!

"You'd be much better off munching on that mouse back at the sewer!" Joker pressed against the garage door and sank to the ground. "I'd pretty much taste like cardboard."

The cat moved closer with its squinty yellow eyes locked on its prey. "Why don't you let me be the judge of that!" he growled.

Joker turned away. He curled up in a ball and covered his eyes just as the garage door rumbled. It made a horrible *clackety-clack* sound, and as it rose, a red-headed boy with a rusty blue bike appeared on the other side. The cat let out a hiss and scurried off, Joker tumbled backward, hitting his head on the cement. Suddenly, everything was spinning. He closed his eyes, snapped his fingers, and morphed back into a card.

"Awesome!" the young boy squealed. His mouth and hands were covered in chocolate, and when he leaned down to pick Joker up, a long glistening thread of drool landed on him.

"Ugh, gross!" Joker screamed. He tried to wipe the brown sticky goop from his face when he eyed a large clothespin coming toward him. It sprang open like the jaws of an alligator and then snapped shut, trapping his arms and torso.

Poor Joker struggled to wriggle himself free. He pleaded and hollered, but the boy heard nothing. He clipped Joker to the fork of his bicycle wheel and sped away. Joker fluttered helplessly as the bike zipped down the road, past the cat, and over the bridge. The boy pedaled quickly, taking great pleasure in making his new card snap faster and faster. Minutes turned to hours as he flew through puddles, around hedges, and over craggy paths. Wind and brush flew by while a constant *thrat-tat-tat-tat* rang in Joker's head.

By the time the boy skidded to a halt, Joker was so parched he could barely let out a yelp. But soon, the dust settled. The boy leaned his bike against a fire hydrant, grabbed his baseball glove, and disappeared. Joker dropped his head, weary but relieved. That was, until a Chihuahua with stumpy legs and long whiskers pranced by.

The dog sniffed his way along the side of the hydrant, across the bike, and over to Joker. Joker's eyes shot open. He watched in horror as the dog paused, backed up, and lifted his leg just above him.

"Oh, heavens. NO!" Joker cried.

The Chihuahua spun around and stared at Joker's card for a long moment. All at once, he lunged forward and grabbed him with his tiny white teeth. Joker nearly had a heart attack.

"Ow!" Joker yelped. "Ow, ow, wow, wow, wow!"

The dog jerked and pulled. He tugged on Joker's card until he finally came free, and they both tumbled across the sidewalk. In a flash, Joker gave a snap and jumped to his feet. He stood there rubbing the back of his neck.

The dog moved closer. "Your English, it's not so good!" he said. "It's bow-wow-wow. NOT ow, ow, wow. BOW-WOW-WOW!" He took his time and annunciated slowly, "BUUH—BUUH—BUUH."

Joker's eyes turned to slits as the Chihuahua's cheeks puffed in and out like a blowfish.

"My name Ferdinand, like thee bull!" He quivered. "What's your name?"

The sight of this strange little rat of an animal was really beginning to irritate Joker. His bulbous eyes were far too big for their sockets, and his body shook like it was standing on a spinning washing machine. But as Joker gazed at the bike—its wheels covered in muck—he suddenly realized what this dog had done for him. He stumbled forward and raised his trembling hand to his chest. He tried to introduce himself, but after such a harrowing ride, his tongue would only wag from side to side. Joker began to whimper.

Ferdinand moved closer. "I too was young pup in a strange land. So, so alone." He shook his head sadly. "Now, I make my own way. Not everyone wants an old stray like me." He blinked his giant brown eyes at Joker. "You are tired my little friend, yes?"

Joker wiped his tears and nodded.

Ferdinand pounced forward and dropped his front legs. "Come, I give you ride."

Joker felt numb. His head throbbed. He was quite sure his tongue was broken. Mud and bramble caked his fine silk clothes. Even so, his thoughts shifted to his friends trapped behind the Cider Shoppe. More than ever, he was determined to find Alex. "Yes, ride good." He shut his eyes and tried to pull his words together. "My friends." Joker sniveled. "They're in terrible trouble. I need to find Alex!" He grabbed onto Ferdinand's collar and hoisted himself onto the little dog's back. They took a few steps into the bright afternoon sun. Joker looked to his left, then his right. "This way," he said. And they galloped off.

WALK OF SHAME

Alex sat on the hard oak bench outside the principal's office contemplating his fate while the office secretary banged on her printer.

"This darn thing just keeps jamming!" she grumbled.

The harder she smacked the side of the machine, the more consumed he became with worry. Alex covered his face with his hands. Horrible thoughts churned in his head like a brewing storm. Was Principal Gorman going to give him detention, or even worse—would he be expelled? What if he and Mr. Schnitzer were in his office calling his mom at this very moment? Or, maybe they were calling the police! Where were his cards? Who could have taken his cards?

The door from the lobby swung open. It was Mrs. Logan. She stepped briskly past the secretary and sat down beside Alex.

"What happened?" she whispered.

Alex lowered his eyes. "I don't know. Mr. Schnitzer hates me. He's always on my case!"

"Well, is it true? Were you trying to leave school?"

Alex sighed. "Yes, it's just—my cards were stolen after the tournament, and I've been trying to find them all week. They were my father's."

"Oh Alex, I'm so sorry. Who would have done such a thing?"

He shook his head. "I don't know."

Mrs. Logan sat quietly for a moment then jumped up and marched into Principal Gorman's office unannounced. Alex watched as she shut the door. At first, it was quiet. Then he heard voices. Loud voices. He tried to make out the silhouettes behind the mottled glass. It was easy to figure out who Mrs. Logan was. Mr. Schnitzer was obvious, too. He was the one who looked like he was trying to fly—his arms flailing in every direction. Principal Gorman was the taller one who was nodding. Everything turned quiet. Was Principal Gorman patting Mr. Schnizter on the back? Maybe he just won some kind or award for catching the most delinquents. That couldn't be good news for Alex. He swallowed hard as the door opened.

"Alex, would you please come in here?" Mrs. Logan asked.

Alex's knees felt wobbly. For a moment, he was afraid if he stood up, his legs would give way like two twigs about to snap. He held onto the bench's armrest and took a deep breath before making his way into the office.

Mrs. Logan stood by his side. Mr. Schnitzer remained in the corner by the window. His beloved whistle dangled from his neck, glimmering in the afternoon light.

"I am not condoning your behavior today young man," Principal Gorman cautioned.

"Yes sir," Alex answered, suddenly aware of the file on the principal's desk with his name printed in capital letters.

"I'll bet he was trying to cut science class. I hear there's a test today!" Mr. Schnitzer snapped.

Alex cringed. Mr. Burroughs' exam! He had been warning the class about it for weeks. With everything that was going on, Alex had totally forgotten it was today.

"Mrs. Logan thinks we should give you another chance," Principal Gorman said, tapping his pen on the desk. Just then, the school bell rang. "Mr. Schnitzer will escort you to your science class. You are not to leave the school premises until the final bell rings. Do you understand?"

"Yes, Principal Gorman, I understand." Alex nodded quickly. "It won't happen again."

Alex turned to leave. He and Mrs. Logan exchanged a quick smile. Although Alex was thankful she had come to his aid, his relief was short-lived once he realized he was about to endure the most uncomfortable walk of his life to Mr. Burroughs' class.

The walk felt like a mile. Not a word was spoken, but Alex could tell by the way Mr. Schnitzer's nostrils flared that he wasn't at all happy with the outcome of the meeting. Had it been up to him, Alex was sure he would have conjured up a more suitable punishment, like a ten-mile hike around the track, or the equivalent in push-ups!

All eyes were on Alex once they arrived at Mr. Burroughs' science class. His face turned beet red as Mr. Schnitzer followed, inches from his heels, all the way down the aisle to his seat by the window. Mr. Burroughs trailed behind them. He peered over his smudged spectacles and handed Alex the exam. Crammed in the corner, the two teachers hovered while Alex fumbled though his backpack in search of a pencil.

Mr. Schnitzer leaned close. "You may have Principal Gorman fooled, but I'll be watching you like a hawk from here on in. Count on it!"

Alex shrank in his chair with his eyes glued on Mr. Schnitzer as he marched up the aisle and out the door. That's when he noticed the rest of the class staring in his direction.

The test, as it turned out, wasn't anywhere near as difficult as Mr. Burroughs had warned. It was mostly Q&A on a subject Alex knew well—planets located within the asteroid belt. Just before he left Ridge Park, he had plans to construct a mini solar system with his buddies in the science club. They even took a trip to the planetarium in Manhattan, but they never had a chance to create it. Even so, Alex studied it enough that he pretty much had the vast order of the Universe memorized.

He finished the test quickly, carefully drawing each planet's position and naming them before handing it to Mr. Burroughs. As he walked back to his desk and waited for the last period to end, he couldn't help thinking about his cards. He had to keep searching. With ten minutes left to class, he pulled out his notebook and started drawing a map of all the locations he had been.

"Alex!"

Alex looked up. Everyone was still working on the exam. For a second, he thought he saw a dog pop up in the window. He turned to see if anyone else had noticed, then he went back to his map.

"Alex!"

The dog's head appeared again. Alex wasn't a fool. Someone, namely Dylan, was probably playing another cruel joke on him. He tried to ignore it, but the sight of the dog's face repeatedly appearing then disappearing from the window made him laugh. Alex's amusement faded when he heard his name again.

"Alex."

I know that voice, he thought.

Whoever it was, screamed long and loud over the school bell. "ALEXAAAAAANDER!"

Alex finally leaned out the window. There, on the school lawn, was a sight he would not soon forget.

Doggy in the Window

A scruffy dog with large saucer eyes and perky ears, gazed up at him. Alex felt his heart melt. Then he spotted Joker straddled on the dog's back, waving his arms over his head as if he were trying to stop a speeding train. Alex grabbed his backpack and raced out of the building.

"Joker, where have you been?" he said, glancing over his shoulder at the students pouring out of the main entrance. He led Joker and the dog behind a bush and dropped to his knees. "I've been wor—"

"You will not believe the harrowing experience I just had!" Joker interrupted.

"Where is everybody else?" Alex asked.

"Do you know I was nearly recycled?"

"Where is everybody?"

"Then this huge wave. And that psycho kitty!" Joker shook his head.

"WHERE IS EVERYONE?" Alex slammed his backpack to the ground.

Joker jumped. "Okay, okay. We were kidnapped by this hairy pinhead of a guy!"

"What?"

"I am not kidding! Look, this has been the most traumatic experience of my life! And I know what you're thinking, Joker is a bit of, you know—"

"A troublemaker?"

"Well, yes." Joker professed, as he smoothed his torn, tire-marked jacket.

"Obnoxious?"

"Hmmm, perhaps." Joker flicked the crusty mud from his pants.

"One who is known to exaggerate the truth?" Alex announced, folding his arms.

"You're right, Alex, okay? You're right!" Joker hid his face in the bend of his arm.

Alex suddenly felt bad for being so straightforward. Then, Joker's head sprang up.

"Huhhh! Maybe I'm dying. I've been getting these awful migraines, you know."

Right there on the school lawn, Joker began to test his vision. He closed one eye, then the other. He clamped his wrist with his fingers and checked his pulse. Joker gazed at the clouds and studied the building's stonework, but it quickly became impossible to avoid the look of frustration on Alex's face. Joker lowered his head.

"I just. I guess nobody ever . . ."

Alex sighed. "Nobody ever what?"

"Nobody ever pays any attention to me. Even that Theo guy threw me out. I'm pointless!" Joker kicked the grass with his boot. "I'm not even needed in a game of Poker! I'm just a joke!" He looked at Emilio's tiny face pouting back at him. "No. No really. I am! I'm just a big fat joke!"

Alex listened quietly. He was touched by Joker's honesty. "Look, Joker, I know you don't mean any harm. Wouldn't it be so much easier if you just thought before you spoke? Rather than react like a . . . a—"

"Clown?" Joker hunched his shoulders.

"Isn't it possible everyone would appreciate you for who you are?"

Joker wiped his nose with his sleeve. "You're right, Alex, I'm really. Truly. Sorry." He sniffed. "But you have to believe me. When you were signing autographs, this guy came over and grabbed us off the table and kidnapped us to the Cider Shoppe."

"Right. The Cider Shoppe. If you say so," Alex snapped. Hadn't Joker listened to a single word he'd said?

"Well, not exactly the Cider Shoppe. It's more like a secret room in the back."

Alex's face fell. "What kind of secret room?"

"You know, where they play card games for lots of money. Oh, it was awful! Trust me when I tell you. It was a dump! It makes your room look like a spa. The worst part is the King and Queen—all the suits—are being used to con people. It's not good, Alex. These two guys, Theo and Mr. Raymond, are planning some kind of scam!"

Alex's stomach churned. How could he have let this happen?

"A secret room?" a voice behind him asked.

Alex shot around. Lindsay was kneeling behind him scratching the little dog's belly.

"No, I mean, yeah—I mean, I don't know." Alex's brain hurt. "I have to find the Cider Shoppe."

"I know that place," she said. "My family owns the pizzeria around the corner from them. It's so cute, the way they have that little man in the window." She moved jerkily like a robot. "Why? What's going on there?"

"I think they stole my cards."

"The ones your dad left you?"

"Yeah," Alex said.

"That's so weird. Why would the Cider Shoppe want to steal your cards?"

"I don't know. I think there may be some kind of illegal activity going on in the backroom." Just uttering those words sent a chill down Alex's spine. He jumped to his feet. "I've gotta go."

"Wait! I'll come with you," Lindsay said. "My father would kill me if he found out, but you really shouldn't go there alone."

Alex hesitated. He could think of a million reasons why he should take care of this himself. The first of which was standing just behind Lindsay, beating the dust from his tiny jacket. As it was, Lindsay didn't believe him when he said his cards had magic powers. How would he ever explain talking to a four-inch-tall know-it-all that only he could see?

"Look, I know this place isn't, you know, New York," Lindsay said. "But, I'm pretty sure there may be a few of us cool kids in the mix." She pushed her hair behind her ears and gave him a smile. "Maybe I can help."

Alex grabbed his backpack. He turned toward the street wondering what kind of people would kidnap his friends. Was it just the two men Joker had told him about? Or were there more? The truth was he had no idea what he was up against.

Alex turned to Lindsay, her face filled with concern. "Come on," he said. "Let's go."

As they headed to the Cider Shoppe, Joker jumped onto Ferdinand's back and whispered in the little dog's ear. "Do I look pale to you?"

THE PLAN

The brass sleigh bell above the large red door of the Cider Shoppe rang out as customers entered and left with jugs of the town's favorite potion. Alex and Lindsay stood by the entrance of the alleyway.

"I drink that stuff with breakfast!" Alex confessed.

"Me too!" Lindsay said, staring down the alleyway. "Now that I'm here, I feel like there's something really spooky about this place."

Alex stepped over a broken chair propped beside a dumpster. His eyes locked on something scurrying down the narrow path. "I know what you mean," he said, as it darted beneath a pile of wooden crates.

All at once, the Chihuahua took off after it. Straddled on Ferdinand's back, Joker grabbed onto his collar while the dog raced through the alleyway, digging his snout between the stacks of crates like a pig in search of truffles.

"What's going on here?"

Alex and Lindsay both jumped.

"Whoa! Uh, hi Dad." Lindsay laughed nervously. "Boy you scared me!"

"I should hope so," he said, glaring at Alex. "I was on my way to the store to get more garlic when I saw you two standing here."

Lindsay's father—dressed in a snappy white chef's jacket, a tall pleated hat, and checkered pants—stood with his arms folded. His eyes shifted between the two of them.

"This is Alex, Dad. He's a friend from school."

He looked straight at Alex and then nodded toward the alleyway. "So . . . what's so interesting down there?"

"Oh, uh, nothing really!" Alex answered a little too quickly. He felt the Chihuahua back at his feet, gnawing at his shoelaces. He glanced at the dog, grabbed him, and cradled him in his arms. "My dog," he stammered. "We were playing. Fetch, that is. We were playing fetch, and his ball rolled down that alleyway."

Lindsay's father pulled Joker's card from beneath Ferdinand's collar. "What's this?"

Alex cleared his throat. "Oh, uh, I've been looking for that! Thanks." He took Joker and tucked him in his shirt pocket. "This crazy dog grabs all my stuff!" Sweat trickled down Alex's temples. He patted Ferdinand's head so hard he began to growl.

"So, I guess we'll be heading to the library now," Lindsay announced. She spun around in the direction of the street.

"I don't think so," her father said.

"What?" Lindsay said.

"They don't allow dogs at the library. Just service dogs. I don't imagine Fido here would qualify."

"It's Ferdinand!" Joker sang from Alex's pocket. "Like the bull!"

"Ferdinand," Alex said. "His name is Ferdinand."

"I don't imagine Ferdinand here is a service dog, now is he?"

Alex shook his head slowly.

"Well, then, perhaps you should take him home." Lindsay's father turned to his daughter. "And I will walk you to the library."

Neither Alex nor Lindsay said a word as her father escorted her across the street. Weaving their way through traffic, Lindsay looked over her shoulder. "I'm sorry," she mouthed before she disappeared into the crowd.

Joker climbed onto Alex's shoulder. "Wow! For a minute there, I was sure he knew where we were going!"

"I don't think so," Alex said. But just to make sure, he waited a while before he and Joker ventured down the alleyway.

"This one, Alex. This one. Right here!" Joker pointed to the open window lined with metal bars.

Alex grabbed an empty garbage can and turned it over. He climbed on top and slowly raised his head above the sill. Gray swirls of smoke hung over the room like a blanket. Eight men sat at a large oval table tossing poker chips into the center. There, scattered among piles of money and jewels, were his dearest friends being hurled and slapped across the table.

Alex clenched his fist. All he could do was whisper, "No!"

"What do you see, what's going on?" Joker crawled onto the sill beside him.

"Shhh," Alex said, his eyes fixed on the gamblers.

One of the men waved the Queen of Hearts like a flag, as if to torment one of the other players. Alex could tell she was upset by the look on her face. Her brow was furrowed, and she held on to the edge of her card as if she were on some kind of crazy roller coaster ride.

"I know you've been wantin' this lady for a while now, so I'll tell ya what . . ." The man laughed.

"Put her down. Just put her down!" Alex murmured.

"Whatcha got, Mr. Raymond?" another player said.

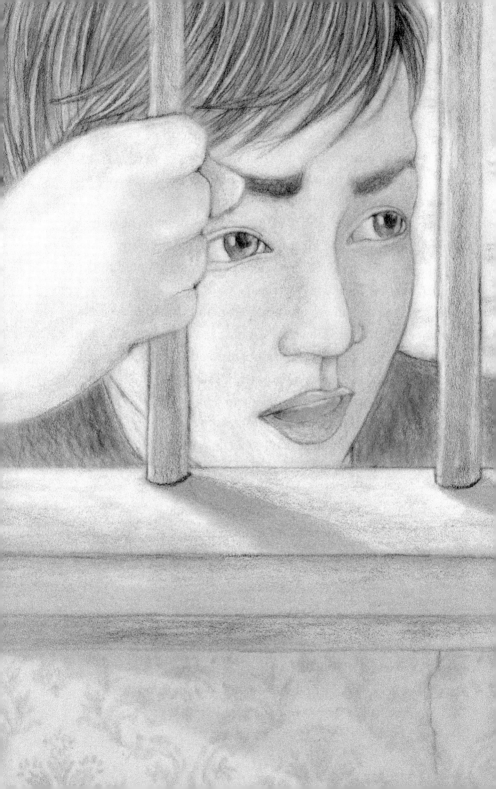

"I gotcha beat. That's all I can tell ya." Mr. Raymond howled with laughter and threw his cards on the table. The other men sank in their chairs while he took a puff of his cigar and leaned over to collect his winnings.

"I've got to get them out of there!" Alex's voice cracked. He pressed his head against the cold brick and shut his eyes tight. In that moment, the letter his father had left him came flooding back.

That is why I am leaving you this extraordinary deck of cards. Take great care of them and they will do the same for you. Remember, Alexander, you have a gift. Only you can hear these cards and see them come to life. No other person will have this ability. Even so, you must be extremely cautious with them, because these cards hold magic for whoever uses them.

Alex felt weak. He was just a few feet away, but it might as well have been a million miles. He sat on the garbage can cradling his head in his hands. The sound of clinking poker chips echoing through the alley was a constant reminder of his carelessness. "What am I going to do?"

"Just go in and grab them!" Joker said.

Alex sat straight. "How can I do that? Once they saw me, they'd come looking for me! That would be crazy. Besides, what kind of danger would I be putting my mom in?" He got back on the garbage can and peered inside. "I just can't take that kind of chance. Not with these guys."

"Well, what if you broke in?" Joker asked.

Alex tugged on one of the metal bars that ran across the window. "Yeah, right. They've probably got this place locked up tighter than Fort Knox. Maybe if I could fit between . . ."

Alex's eyes grew wide. "Wait a minute!" His gaze shifted back and forth as if he were watching a movie in his head. "Maybe I can do this."

"Well, that's a relief." Joker leaned against the brick wall. "I was starting to run out of—"

"The Dance of Suits! That's the answer." Alex said.

Joker rolled his eyes. "Oh, that's hilarious!" He turned to Emilio and laughed, then choked, then laughed again. He stopped long enough to notice the serious look on Alex's face. "Come on now, you can't be serious."

"Why wouldn't it work?" Alex asked.

"Well, for starters, remember your father's letter? The cards hold magic for whoever uses them!" Joker studied his fingernails. "I personally find this a tad offensive."

Alex jumped back on top of the garbage can. "I'm close enough. If Mr. Raymond steps out of the room, I'll be closer to the cards than he is. They'll have to obey me—right?"

"But Alex!" Joker whispered.

"Think about it. If I can get them to dance between these bars . . ." He grabbed hold of the bars and peeked inside just as the cards were tossed in another round. "It'll work. It has to work!" Alex tightened his grip until his knuckles turned white.

"But Alexander!" Joker pleaded.

"I just wish I had more time," Alex murmured. He squatted below the window and shut his eyes. Slowly, he began to navigate his hands through the air—up and over, down and around—trying to remember the sequence of events his father performed onstage.

Joker leapt into his hand and waved his scepter, Emilio, in his face. "Hell-oooo!"

Alex opened his eyes.

"Okay, how can I say this nicely? We performed The Dance, and it was an epic failure. In a nutshell, we stink at it!" Joker said. "We barely started practicing it again. And Jack? He's as nervous as a long-tailed cat in a room full of rocking chairs when it comes to that trick!"

Alex grabbed Joker. "It *will* work. It has to!"

Alex raised himself just beneath the window. "Look, I need you to sneak back inside and tell His Majesty, the Queen, and Jack to get everyone ready for The Dance. We'll wait for these guys to take a break. That's when I'll give the signal." Alex curled his lips and gave a low whistle. "Tell them to listen for the whistle and watch for me in the window. I'll take it from there. Got it?"

"Yes, yes, I understand." Joker nodded.

Joker climbed between the bars and scurried to the end of the sill. He grabbed the curtain cord, wrapped his foot in the line, and disappeared down the side of the wall as if he were descending a cliff.

ROYAL TREATMENT

Mr. Raymond held the perfect hand—King Anton, Jack, the Ace of Hearts, the Ten of Hearts, and Queen Olivia.

The Queen leaned from her card, her hair disheveled and her crown askew. "Well! I don't know what kind of trick that was, but I may need a helmet if they want me to do it again! Do either of you happen to know what all that was about?"

"Yes, my dear, this is a little different from what Alex does," the King said.

"I can see that!"

Mr. Raymond fiddled with his chips, letting them rattle between his fingers. "It's Nick's turn to act."

"Ahhhh." The Queen smiled. "So they're thespians!"

"Mom," Jack said, waving cigar smoke from his face. "I seriously don't think they're acting. These guys mean business!"

The King reached out from his card and patted the Queen's hand. "Hmmm, not quite thespians, Olivia." He scanned the faces at the table. "But I suppose you could call them characters! See this character right here?" The King pointed straight up into Mr. Raymond's hairy nostrils. "He's in charge of us now. Until Alex finds us, we have no choice but to obey his wishes."

Queen Olivia rubbed her head. "Apparently, he wishes to give me a concussion!"

"Olivia dear, Jack is right," the King said. "And these guys mean business. I don't even want to imagine what's in store for us if we don't do as they say. Right now, our only job is to make sure Mr. Raymond ends up with royalty in his hands. By the end of the game, all those chips heaped in the middle of the table must absolutely, unequivocally be piled in front of him. Just follow my lead, and we'll be fine!"

The Queen studied Mr. Raymond's face for a moment then leaned toward the towering stacks of chips. "I see. All those chips for one person?" She straightened her skirt and folded her hands firmly. "A gentleman with any modicum of class would share them with the rest of the table," she huffed.

King Anton climbed from his card and leaned over the top as if he were about to announce from a podium. "People! May I have your attention please!" he shouted to the deck scattered amongst the players. "It pains me to say this, but until further notice, while we are forced into this most unsavory situation, we have no choice but to obey Mr. Raymond's wishes. So here are the rules. . . ." The King reached under his robe and pulled out a tiny manual. He gave his thumb a lick then quickly flipped through its pages. "In order for Mr. Raymond to win every game, we must offer him the royal treatment. Diamonds, listen carefully. In the next round, make sure Mr. Raymond ends up with your highest ranking top five performers—Ace, King, Queen, Jack and Ten. Clubs, you'll follow Diamonds after the next hand. Spades, you'll follow Clubs."

"What about the rest of us?" The Six of Diamonds shouted from across the table.

King Anton waved his arms. "Disperse, man, disperse. Just keep away from your first cousins and you'll be fine!"

"I can't believe we have to obey this creep!" Jack said.

"We have no choice, son. You know as well as I do that while we're in his possession, we have to perform. I just hope . . ."

Before he could finish his thought, King Anton spotted Joker sliding down the curtain cord. He slipped out of Mr. Raymond's hand, and with a snap of his fingers, somersaulted onto the floor to meet him.

"My friend," the King said, placing his hand on Joker's shoulder.

Joker took a moment to catch his breath then asked, "Are you okay, Your Majesty?"

"For now." The King flicked cigar ashes from the front of his robe. "And you? Are you all right?"

"Yes." Joker nodded, gazing at his own filthy attire. "I'm fine, but I am desperately in need a new wardrobe, these are all—"

"And Alex?" the King interrupted. "Does he know we've been card-napped?"

"Yes. He's very upset about this whole mess. He knows you're here and he's working on a way to get you out."

No sooner had Joker begun to share Alex's plan with the King when Mr. Raymond's hand swooped beneath the table and grabbed them. In a flash, they turned back into cards.

"I thought we got rid of this?" Mr. Raymond mumbled. He stepped over to the window and tossed Joker into the alley.

"Listen for the whistle! Then wait for Alex's command!" Joker shouted.

Alex pressed himself against the side of the building while Joker fluttered through the air like a feather floating in the breeze.

"Do you believe this?" Joker whined. He slid to a bumpy halt on the cobblestone, jumped to his feet, and stood there with his arms out. "They threw me out—again!"

"Shhhh. Calm down!" Alex whispered.

"Is it me?" He sniffed under his arms. "Be straight with me Alex. It's me—right?"

"You're fine! What happened? Were you able to speak with them? Are they okay?"

"They're okay." Joker yanked at his jacket. "A bit shaken, but they're ready when you are."

"What about Jack? Did you speak with him, too?"

"Actually no. I couldn't get to him." Joker's eye began to twitch. "That hairy ape grabbed me before I had a chance." He stared up at the window. "Don't worry Alex. I think those pinheads were about to take a break. I'm quite confident His Majesty is relaying the plan as we speak."

"Oh no no no no no!" Jack waved his hands as if he were swatting a fly. He stepped away from the King and Queen and stumbled into a pile of poker chips. "Why doesn't anybody listen to me? Alex knows I can't do this!"

The King and Queen gave each other a look then each grabbed him by an arm.

"But you must!" King Anton said, pulling Jack to his feet. "There are no other options. The Dance of Suits is a team effort. You know that. We need each other to make it work!"

Queen Olivia nodded. "Listen Jack, you are a tremendous athlete. We must motivate each other to do our very best, and sometimes that means pushing ourselves beyond what we think is our best. We would never ask you to do anything we felt you couldn't accomplish." She raised his chin with her gloved hand and said in a most loving voice, "We believe in you. So does Alex!"

Jack brushed himself off. He glared at the soaring piles of poker chips that surrounded them like chimneystacks. He would have done anything to avoid performing The Dance of Suits, and now, they were all relying on him more than ever.

MISDIRECTION

Outside, Alex and Joker waited patiently through the next round. They peered through the window preparing to perform The Dance between the metal bars while one at a time the men at the table threw their cards down. Mr. Raymond gingerly spread his cards in front of him for all to see then leaned back in his seat, grinning.

"You are one lucky bum!" the man in the denim shirt said. He pushed his chair from the table, grabbed his jacket and left the room. The others followed. They shuffled past Theo, who locked the door behind them just as Mr. Raymond began to count their winnings.

"They're coming!" Alex whispered loudly.

Just then, the alley door jiggled. Joker dove into Alex's shirt pocket once Alex hit the ground. He scooped Ferdinand in his arms and scrambled behind a pile of wooden crates. They crouched there, peeking through the slats as the men stepped into the alley and paused beneath the light of the window. Alex's heart pounded. He held the dog close and clamped its snout tightly when it started to growl. Once the men disappeared in the early evening fog, Alex climbed back on top of the garbage can.

Mr. Raymond divided their newly won cash into neat little piles. "How many games have we played with this deck?"

Theo gazed at the ceiling. "Hmmm . . . about twelve."

"And how many games have we won?"

Theo looked up again, "Hmmm . . . about twelve."

"Indeed." Mr. Raymond folded his hands and grinned.

Theo laughed. "What are the odds?"

"There's nothing odd about it." Mr. Raymond grabbed a stack of bills and ran his thumb along the edge. "I do believe we have all the makings of a magic deck!"

Theo gathered up the cards. "Yeah, today was a good one!"

"I'll say." Mr. Raymond smirked. "One second I was holding a bunch of twos and threes, and then poof! I had me a royal flush." He sashayed beside the safe and opened it. "You know, Theo," he said, patting the massive steel box as if it were his favorite pet. "You and I are about to embark on a golden opportunity." He looked around at the worn seat cushions and peeling wallpaper. "Nothing would make me happier than shutting the Cider Shoppe down and leaving this dinky town for good."

"Where would we go?"

"Vegas!" Mr. Raymond's eyes grew wild. "I can see it clear as day. There'd be tall palm trees, marble stairways, and huge spotlights that swept across the evening sky. Inside, there'd be hundreds of shiny slot machines and polished mahogany poker tables. The staff would all be dressed in tuxedos and serve those fancy drinks with the tiny umbrellas. And then"—Mr. Raymond wiggled his fingers—"there'd be a stage! The most magnificent stage ever with red velvet curtains and hula girls who'd line up every night and introduce me, Mr. Raymond, as the King! The King of Poker Palace!" His teeth glistened through the smoky haze.

"Wait! They have hula girls in Vegas?" Theo mumbled.

Mr. Raymond's smile faded. "Well then"—he cleared his throat—"now that we know these cards are for real, we are all set for the big game tomorrow. What time are our esteemed victims . . . I mean guests, due to arrive?"

Theo pulled a small notebook from his back pocket. "Let's see . . . tomorrow, we have some very special attendees: Andre from Nevada, Carlos from Miami, Merle from Texas, and Vlad from the Ukraine."

"Vlad's in town?"

Theo picked up the phone. "Yeah, he's meeting some of his associates on the east coast. He should be here around noon. I'm gonna confirm with the rest of the boys now."

"Things are looking up my friend." Mr. Raymond rubbed his hands together and carefully placed the stacks of bills alongside the cards in the safe. "With all the collateral we raked in this week, we are going to blow the roof off of this place tomorrow."

Theo hung up the phone. "But what if the cards don't work right tomorrow?"

"Highly improbable," Mr. Raymond said, raising a fresh cigar to his lips.

"Yeah—but what if?"

"What if," Mr. Raymond echoed as he grabbed his lighter. He clicked it a few times and stared at the hissing blue flame. "I would hate to think our enchanted deck here would ever consider betraying us." An evil grin grew on his face. "If they did, I suppose we'd have ourselves a little bonfire!"

"Yeah, right, a bonfire!" Theo snickered.

Mr. Raymond slammed the safe door and spun the combination. "That should keep them safe and sound."

"Hey, that's a good one. *Safe and sound!*"

Alex squatted below the window, horrified. "Nooo! I only needed a few more minutes. I would have had them in my . . ." He dropped his head.

Just then, the window slammed shut. Alex and Joker stared at each other as Mr. Raymond closed the curtains.

"Oh dear, what do we do now?" Joker asked. "What if that window is shut tomorrow?"

Alex slumped on the garbage can. He suddenly felt sick to his stomach. "I don't know. I guess we'll have to find a way inside."

"Don't worry, Alex, everything will be alright," Joker said.

Alex wasn't at all convinced that was the case. In fact, the thought occurred to him that The Dance of Suits could turn into a complete disaster. Then what would he do? His treasured friends forever lost in a world of illegal gambling, prisoners of some sleazy lowlife criminals! How could he live with that burden? As they walked through the alleyway, he quietly agonized over the consequences of his plan when someone yelled, "Watch out!"

Before Alex had a chance to react, a boy on a speeding bicycle blew through the fog and nearly crashed into him. Someone grabbed Alex from behind and yanked him out of the way. They both hit the ground just as the wheels of the bike went racing by, inches from his head. He turned and found Lindsay lying behind him.

"Are you okay?" she asked.

Alex's heart was pounding so fast that he thought it would leap from his chest. "I think so. What are you doing here?"

Lindsay sat up. "Oh man, what a day! Sorry about my father. It took forever to get him out of the library. That ridiculous parade got him going a little cuckoo! He hired more staff, ordered new uniforms, and now he's got way too much time on his hands. He started looking up all these old recipes. I couldn't get him to leave!"

"That's alright," Alex said, rubbing his neck. "Are you okay?"

"Yeah, I guess so." She wiped the front of her pants with her hands. "Someone oughta give that kid driving lessons! What a jerk!"

They both got to their feet and stared as the boy skidded to a halt just outside the poker room. He was wearing a baseball cap and a shiny jacket emblazoned with Dave's Barbeque on the back. He jumped off the bike and grabbed a box of foil-wrapped sandwiches from his basket.

"How'd it go?" Lindsay asked. "Were you able to get your cards?"

"Not exactly."

"What happened?"

"It's a long story. The bottom line is I have to get inside."

"Inside? How are you going to manage that?"

Alex's head was spinning. What possible excuse could he come up with to get inside? And how was he ever going to do it without being recognized? The only thing he could think of was going in through the Cider Shoppe entrance. But that didn't really make any sense. He needed to go in through the back door where the gamblers came and went. He had to look like he belonged there. There *had* to be a way!

He was trying to figure out his next move when his eyes fell on the bright red letters of the boy's jacket. Suddenly, it came to him. He turned to Lindsay. "Wait! Did you say uniforms?"

"Yeah, you know, like what my Dad was wearing—white jacket, red kerchief, checkered pants, really silly hat." She laughed. "He's even got the delivery boys wearing them. He's all into branding. Whatever that is!"

"Lindsay, do you think I could borrow one of those uniforms tomorrow? I'll need a couple of pizzas too." He reached in his pocket for the few dollars he had.

"I guess so, why?"

"I can't go in there like this. I need a disguise."

She looked at him, puzzled.

"It's called misdirection. . . . It's a magic term. Better they look at the hat and not me. You think you can do that?"

She waved his money away. "Only if I can join you." She grinned excitedly. "I'd kinda like to see what a magic card really looks like up close." She winked.

Alex knew she still didn't believe him. The truth was she may never believe him, but at least she was trying to help. Now, more than ever, Alexander Finn needed all the help he could get.

"What time?" Lindsay asked.

Alex turned back to the delivery boy just in time to see him ring the bell three times then wait to be let in. "I'm thinking noon . . . right around lunch time," Alex said as the heavy door slammed.

Safe and Sound

The suits fumbled around in the darkness of the safe.

"Olivia, my dear, are you okay?" King Anton asked.

"Yes, I do believe I am," the Queen answered.

"How about you Jack?" he asked.

A loud bang followed. "Ouch! Uh, yes, Father, I'm fine. I'm just trying to find . . . wait! Did I hear those two goons say they would destroy us if we didn't win big bucks for them?"

"I'm sure they were just trying to scare us," the King said.

"Well, it's working! What if I can't do this? I don't think I can do this."

"We can't afford another slip up from Jack!" the Ace of Diamonds barked.

"You said it!" the Nine of Spades shouted.

"This is terrible!" the Three of Clubs whined.

Their little voices began to rise with concern.

"Listen up!" King Anton clapped. "We all just need to calm down. Look, everything's going to be fine. Alex knows we're here. We just have to keep doing what we've been doing until he finds a way—"

"Goodness, it's awfully dark in here, isn't it?" the Queen interrupted.

"It most certainly is!" a soft voice agreed.

Jack jumped. "Who's that?"

A small light flickered from the corner of the safe. It danced between the shadows, slowly illuminating the space in a warm glow until a golden charm bracelet shimmered before them. Jack stood stunned as a delicate ballerina unlinked herself and stepped forward on the tip of her toes. She began to pirouette. With each turn, she grew a little taller, until finally she stood eye to eye with her guests.

"Welcome!" she cooed. The charms behind her rang out like tiny bells as she curtsied for the royal families.

Jack remained silent, mesmerized by her radiant beauty. Her buttery-yellow hair swept upward, and the layers of her skirt floated down like the petals of a flower.

"Forgive me," he said, blinking himself back from his trance. "I seem to have misplaced my manners." He turned to the rest of the suits. "Please allow me to introduce the Diamonds, the Spades, and the Clubs."

"How do you do," they said in unison.

"And these are my parents, King Anton and Queen Olivia." He quietly gazed into the ballerina's eyes. "And uh, oh yes, my name is Jack. Jack of Hearts, that is."

She smiled warmly. "I'm Penelope. It's an honor to meet you all."

"It's lovely to meet you, too," the King said.

Queen Olivia nodded.

"What are you doing in here?" Jack asked.

Penelope dropped her shoulders and sighed. "I guess you've met Mr. Raymond."

"Well, yes. We've had some dealings with him recently."

"He won me in a poker game," she said.

"How long have you been here, my dear?" asked the King.

"Quite a long time." Her chin trembled. "At least a few years."

"Oh my!" The Queen clutched her chest.

"What?" Jack said. "How have you survived in here all alone?"

"Oh!" Penelope's eyes sparkled. "I'm not alone."

A piano, a violin, a paintbrush, and a dragonfly charm surrounded her and began to jingle. Their golden light flickered across the safe as gentle music played.

Penelope moved a few items out of the way and went about preparing a number of beds for her guests. "Mr. Raymond comes by late in the morning."

Jack couldn't take his eyes off her as she plumped stacks of hundred-dollar bills and covered each with a soft black velvet jewelry pouch.

"This should keep you all comfortable for a while."

"Thank you," the King said.

"We are rather tired." The Queen yawned.

She guided the Diamonds and Spades to their pouches in one corner and the Clubs and Hearts to their pouches in the other. After she made a special bed for King Anton and Queen Olivia, she set off to the other side of a tall stack of bills to make a bed for Jack.

"Just so you know, we plan on being out of here tomorrow," Jack said.

Penelope paused. "Oh, that's too bad!" She slapped her hand over her mouth. "Oh dear, that didn't come out right at all. Of course, you want to get out as soon as possible. Forgive me. It's just that I've been in here so long that I've forgotten what it feels like to dance in the moonlight. And your company is, well . . . wonderful!"

Jack's face felt warm when she looked deep into his eyes. "I guess you don't get the chance to dance very often," he said, glancing around.

The charms nudged closer. "I dance every day." Penelope closed her eyes and began to sway. "Just listen to that sweet sound. Who could stop themselves?" She lifted her arm and held her invisible partner while the violin and piano's soulful melody swept her in circles across the safe. "Do you dance, Jack?"

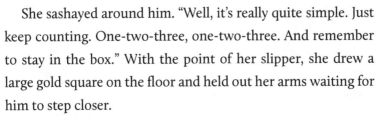

Jack took a deep breath. "I'm actually a terrible dancer."

Penelope stopped dead in her tracks. "Come now. The son of a king must know how to dance!"

"No." He shook his head quickly.

She sashayed around him. "Well, it's really quite simple. Just keep counting. One-two-three, one-two-three. And remember to stay in the box." With the point of her slipper, she drew a large gold square on the floor and held out her arms waiting for him to step closer.

Jack studied the shimmering diagram glowing beneath his feet. He stepped closer, awkwardly taking her hand in his. At first, all he could do was stare at the floor and count to three in his head. Moments later, they were gliding long and wide between stacks of bills. They dipped and spun until, suddenly, they stumbled into a pouch of diamonds and fell back laughing.

"See you're a natural!" she said.

"Hardly." Jack grinned. He couldn't help staring at her golden locks and the tiny wisps of hair that caught the light. "How is it that you ended up in here?"

Penelope sat up. She tilted her head to the side and ran her fingers across the velvet bag. "I used to belong to a lovely lady. She could do everything—sing, dance, paint, play the violin. Her husband gave me to her on their first anniversary. His name was Peter. Every year after, he gave her another charm for each of her passions. We were like a family, all of us so happy. Then she died, and Peter lost his way. It was quite sad, really. He lost his wife and his home. Then he lost us to Mr. Raymond."

Jack's heart ached as she wiped her tears. He took her hand. "You'll come with us."

"Oh, that would be lovely, but—"

"But what?"

"Haven't you noticed? Mr. Raymond loves to win! He just continues to collect things." She got to her feet and slowly twirled past every corner of the safe. Her warm, golden glow shimmered like a beacon.

Jack's eyes jumped from the stacks of bills, to clusters of gold watches, to bag after bag of velvet pouches overflowing with diamonds and rubies.

Penelope stepped aside. "I don't think he'll have a reason to gamble a gold bracelet away."

Jack wanted to help. He tried to find some consolable words, but his eyes kept drifting to Mr. Raymond's collection.

"It's okay. There's nothing to be said. Why don't you get some sleep," she whispered.

Jack sat on the bed she had made him and watched her disappear to the back of the safe. Squinting through the fading light at the sheer mass of Mr. Raymond's winnings, his chilling threats echoing in Jack's head. Suddenly, he felt dizzy. How could he possibly perform The Dance under that kind of pressure? Jack pulled off his boots and dropped his head. In his heart, he knew that getting out of there safely and back into Alex's hands would surely take a miracle.

SHATTERED

Pieces of Alex's plan spun like planets in his head as he dashed home through the thickening fog. Lindsay had offered to help him with a disguise, but still there was so much more to do. Alex prepared for the long night ahead. He tucked Ferdinand under his jacket and tiptoed upstairs to his room. The dog happily sniffed around while Alex searched his belongings. He rummaged through his dresser drawers. He lifted books and dug through a few of the boxes stacked against the wall. Finally, he found what he was looking for—another deck of cards.

He dropped them on his desk and spread them in a row. How strange it was to see the King's and Queen's blank stares. Alex closed his eyes, his heart filled with regret. Of all the things that could have happened, having his friends in the clutches of a couple of malicious thieves was most unbearable. The fact that Mr. Raymond would even consider destroying his cards if they didn't work worried him the most. One slipup from Jack could have devastating consequences. Alex knew all too well that even in magic there can be flaws—and sometimes flaws can be treacherous.

He tried to shake away the horrible images that kept creeping into his brain. Instead, he focused on the only thing that mattered—piecing together The Dance of Suits. He remembered his father's words as they sat at the kitchen table that very last day. "Build it from the inside out."

Alex took a deep breath and tried to concentrate on making the cards float. Anxious to unleash the power that must have surged through his own father's body, he raised his hands and wiggled his fingers. But the cards remained motionless.

He tightened his muscles, flexing his forearms until they began to cramp. This time, the cards merely shimmied. Alex slammed his hands on the desk and lowered his head. He couldn't help picture his friends trapped in that safe. What had he done? How was he ever going to get this to work?

If there was any chance of summoning the energy he had witnessed in his father when he watched him practice in the middle of the night, Alex had to clear his head of all his negative thoughts. He shut his eyes. He drew deep breaths and concentrated on the tips of his fingers. Over and over, he swept his arms in a circular motion, and over and over the cards quivered then collapsed in a heap.

Alex sank against the wall of boxes. He squeezed his palms into his temples, acutely aware that more than any card trick or illusion he had ever performed, The Dance of Suits required something more—some element that he barely understood. He needed more time, and he knew it.

Outside, the trees cracked and snapped in the wind. The moon shone brightly across his tiny room. The life he once adored was now stacked in cartons so high that their monolith shadow stretched across the floor. In a fit of fury, Alex struck one of the boxes with his fist. Ferdinand let out a whimper and crawled under the bed while Alex punched and kicked, again and again. Books, trophies, and magazines all crashed to the floor with such a thud that his father's photograph slammed down on the desk like a rock. He tried to reach for it, but it was too late. The glass hit the mahogany surface and shattered into a hundred tiny pieces.

"Alex, are you okay?" his mom shouted up the stairs.

"Yeah, Mom, I just tripped. I'm fine."

"Okay. That's it. You and I are taking care of those boxes this week. No more excuses!"

Alex fell into his chair, holding the broken frame. A shard of glass had ripped a corner of the photograph. He tried to piece it together. "I'm so sorry, Dad," he whispered. Tears streamed down his cheeks. "I don't know why all this is happening." Alex ran his finger over the rip and looked deep into his father's face, aching for some kind of sign. "What am I going to do?"

"Alexander Finn," Joker said, stepping over the broken glass. "You are the best magician around, hands down! Tomorrow will work out fine. Even in these shabby, tired clothes, I remain confident."

Alex turned to Joker. "It's just that my father trusted me with you, and now I've ruined everything."

"No, Alex, you haven't ruined anything." Joker climbed onto Alex's shoulder. "You are part of our family, and we are part of yours. Don't you see? We belong together!"

Alex listened to Joker's words. He wiped his tears, grabbed his notebook splayed between the fallen boxes, and began to sketch. He tried to deconstruct The Dance, breaking it down into a series of movements and commands.

The moon arched across the sky as crumpled pages fell like snowballs around him. He drew and redrew until he could no longer hold his head up. Exhausted and overcome, Alex difted off into a deep, disturbing dream.

"DO IT AGAIN!"

Alex was standing in a courtyard in front of an angry mob. The ground looked scorched, and the walls were plastered in cracked cement much too tall to climb. He wiped the sweat from his face as the crowd of strangers taunted him.

"DO IT AGAIN!" they chanted.

A few people lunged forward demanding he perform his floating trick over and over. He tried his best to remember, but his mind blurred in a panic. The mob parted in two, revealing behind them a deep, dark, cavernous hole. Alex tried to shuffle the cards, but his hands shook so badly they slipped through his fingers. He watched in horror as they tumbled into the bottomless pit. Alex dropped to his knees. He tried to grab them, but in a flash, they were gone. Only their desperate screams for help lingered as they disappeared into the abyss.

Hot breath ran down the back of his neck. Alex turned. It was another magician. His black cape swept over Alex like a dark cloud. The magician extended his hand. He slowly unfurled his long chalky fingers, exposing Alex's trembling cards. "Looking for these?" he said.

Alex reached for them, but the magician pulled away. "I'll give them back, but only if you do the trick again!" He laughed.

Alex grabbed his cards and held them to his chest. He struggled to remember the trick, but the crowd sneered and laughed, and he couldn't concentrate.

The magician stepped back and cupped his ear, as though the repeated sound of the cards' tiny screams as they fell into the chasm were a soothing lullaby. "I'm waiting," he sang.

Alex felt sick to his stomach. Doomed to fail, he couldn't bear to watch his cards plummet into the darkness again. He scanned the crowd. His eyes shifted from side to side as they inched closer. He tried to run, but the mob had locked arms. He spun in circles. His heart pounded wildly as the human ring moved closer.

"Alex!" his father whispered.

Alex shot up gasping for air, his face covered in sweat. He was back in his room, but it all looked strangely different. Had he stepped into another dream? All the boxes against his wall had disappeared. Books and lacrosse trophies lined the shelves. The tree outside his window was filled with bright green leaves, as if it he had slept until spring.

"Son . . ."

Alex jumped from his bed. He raced into the hallway and slid to a halt. There, bathed in a violet blue light, stood his father. His arms were outstretched, waiting to greet his son. Alex ran over and held him so tightly his entire body ached. He couldn't remember the last time he felt such perfect happiness. For a long time, they didn't say a word.

His father took him by his shoulders and smiled. His brown eyes sparkled just as they did the last time Alex saw him. Alex beamed when his father pulled a deck of cards from his pocket and shuffled them high above his head.

"It's the element of surprise," his father said, manipulating the cards into flapping wings. "Just when you think the trick is over, it turns around and spins the other way." His powerful hands moved in a broad sweep, turning the cards into a flock of snow-white geese that quickly fluttered off. He snapped his fingers, and the cards reappeared. First in his left hand, then his right, and finally into his son's hands.

The joy that had filled Alex's heart suddenly melted like wax near a flame. He cradled the cards in his hands and slowly walked back into his room. Alex sank on his bed. He wanted to tell his father what had happened. How his cherished deck had been stolen because of his carelessness. He struggled to form the words when his father sat beside him and unclenched his son's fingers. "You must learn to trust your abilities. Let everything fade away, except your natural instincts. It is only then that you will discover the true source of your power."

His father snapped his fingers, and one by one, the cards whirled like tops out of Alex's hands. They twirled through the window and climbed into the purple night, spinning into twinkling stars. Alex fell into a deep sleep as his father's voice faded.

"Remember, Alex, a trick is merely an idea until you breathe life into it. Keep steady. Focus, and the magic will come."

SLEIGHT MISGIVINGS

Saturday morning at twelve noon, whistles blew, cymbals crashed, and the drums began to roll. Under a brilliant blue sky, Orchard's Harvest Parade had officially begun. Across the street, Joker and Ferdinand stood by while Alex paced from one side of the alleyway to the other.

"Am I late?" Lindsay panted, her arms piled high with shopping bags and a large black satchel.

"Right on time. Did you have any trouble?"

"Honestly? I thought I was going to have a major problem with my dad." She handed Alex a few of the bags. "But not today! My father's totally swamped. He's already made like three hundred pies this morning. He never even noticed me!"

"What's this?" He studied the black leather satchel.

"It keeps the pizzas hot."

"Great, the hotter the better." Alex watched the drummers march by. He couldn't help but chuckle.

"What's so funny?"

"Nothing really. It's just . . . this is the last place I ever thought I'd end up right now."

"Yeah." She winced. "Me too. I kind of feel bad because everyone in my family always gets so into it. I just—you know—can't."

Alex studied the residents of Orchard who had gathered along the sidewalks. Some brought folding chairs, others brought thermoses and picnic baskets. As much as he hated being there, there was something to be said for a town that refused to replace their Victorian homes for skyscrapers and parking lots.

"My mom told me how she tried to avoid the parade every year when she was a kid. Now, she's somewhere down by the bleachers writing an article for her paper."

"That's so funny!" Lindsay said. "It's like the stuff you hate the most ends up changing your life . . . you know, in a good way."

Alex thought about that as the band marched up Cortland Boulevard. Since the move, he could think of a number of things he hated, starting with Mr. Schnitzer and Dylan along with his football buddies. Except for meeting Lindsay, he was quite sure none of them would ever end up changing his life—in a good way that is.

The crowd continued to grow along the street while he and Lindsay backed into the alley beside the Cider Shoppe. They slipped behind the dumpsters and jumped to the bottom of the stairwell. Lindsay began pulling out the contents of the shopping bags—a couple of chef's hats, some bright red scarves, and two neatly pressed white jackets.

"I grabbed the smallest ones I could find," she said holding up one of the jackets.

Alex put on the chef's jacket, knotted the scarf, and pushed the silliest hat he'd ever seen firmly on his head. "How do I look?"

Lindsay laughed. "I think we'd better roll up those sleeves."

Alex examined his jacket. It hung a little low, and the sleeves came to his knuckles. He began rolling them up when he noticed Ferdinand pawing at the pizzas.

"No," Alex whispered loudly. "You already ate!"

Ferdinand whined and backed away. He shut his eyes, held his nose high, and sniffed the hot aromas wafting toward him.

"He's a cutie," Lindsay said, buttoning her jacket. "How long have you had him?"

"He's actually not mine."

"Whose is he?"

"He's mine!" Joker shouted from Alex's pocket.

"Ahem!" Alex cleared his throat and put his hand over his pocket. "I don't know. I think he's looking for a home."

Alex climbed out of the stairwell and reached in his back pocket for his regular deck of cards. He glanced around, spread them in a fan, and ran his fingers across their faces.

"What are you doing?" Lindsay asked.

"I'm removing the Joke"—Alex lowered his voice—"I'm removing the Jokers from the deck."

"Um. I can still hear, you know!" Joker scrambled out of Alex's pocket. "People can be so mean," he mumbled to Emilio. He gave Alex a long look then somersaulted onto Ferdinand's back.

"Are you almost ready?" Alex asked.

Lindsay sprang to the top of the stairs. She stood there with her arms out. "Do I look okay?"

Alex's face fell.

She ran her hand over her jacket. "What's wrong?"

A sinking feeling suddenly came over him. He had already placed his cards in terrible danger, now he was afraid he was about to do the same to Lindsay. He couldn't imagine having that happen.

His voice turned serious. "Lindsay, 1 really appreciate you doing this, but maybe it's not the best idea for you to come inside."

Lindsay looked him in the eye. "Listen, I don't know if these cards have magic powers or not. What 1 do know is they mean a lot to you, and 1 really want to help. Isn't that what friends do?"

"Yeah." Alex lowered his head and smiled. "1 have to admit I'm kind of glad you're here. Just . . . listen, if at any point you get scared, 1 want you to leave. Promise?"

"1 promise."

Alex grabbed the pizza satchel. The truth was, he really was glad she was there, but saying it out loud made him feel even better.

Once they reached the back entrance of the Cider Shoppe, they stood there for a long moment, eyeing the massive steel door and the window thick with metal bars. Alex stepped forward and rang the bell three times.

"Let's do some magic," he said.

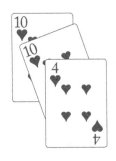

JACKPOT

The cramped entrance reeked of stale cigars. Once the door shut, everything turned a blinding gray. Alex stood there, waiting for his eyes to adjust, while just down the hallway, the Cider Shoppe hummed with activity. *How creepy,* he thought, *to have Orchard customers buying cider just a few feet away, unaware of what's really going on in the back of the building.*

A *clink-clink-clinking* sound filled the corridor. He nudged Lindsay, then tapping his ear with his finger, he pointed to a partially open door a few feet away. The clinking grew louder as they stepped closer. Very quietly, he placed the satchel on the floor and pulled out the pizza boxes.

A thin tangle of smoke churned above the six men seated at the table. Mr. Raymond sat at the head. His eyes bounced from one man to the next like ping-pong balls. He leaned over and pushed a pile of chips into the center.

"Dah!" the man on to his right said. He murmured something in a language that Alex had never heard. He slipped a large gold watch from his wrist, studied his opponents for a moment, and then slowly nudged the watch into the middle of the table. Alex wondered if that was Vlad, their international guest.

"Whoa!" Lindsay whispered. "So these guys are like . . . real criminals?"

"Yeah." Alex wiped the sweat beading up on his face.

"I'm not sure I understand. Why aren't we just grabbing the cards and making a run for it?"

Alex glanced at her for a moment then peeked into the room again. "If I just grab them, they'll know I have the cards. The last thing I want is for Mr. Raymond or Theo to come looking for them again." Alex balanced the pizza boxes on his shoulder. "But, if I can sneak in and replace them, without them knowing, they'll just think the cards have lost their magic powers. They won't have a clue. Got it?"

Lindsay's eyes lit up. "Oh, I get it. So, you're throwing this regular deck on the table and taking yours back?"

Alex sighed. "I wish it were that easy." He nodded toward the poker table where his cards were scattered among the players. "I'll never have time to run around and replace them all. These guys are sharp. I'll only have seconds."

"What are you going to do?"

Alex adjusted his hat. "Hope for a miracle." He took a long, deep breath and pushed the door open.

He made his way across the room to the other side of the table. Alex wanted to sound commanding, as if there was nothing strange about him being there. But then he opened his mouth to speak, and his voice cracked. He froze. That's when he realized the men were so wrapped up in their game that they weren't even paying attention to him. He moved closer to Mr. Raymond.

"So, uh—where would you like us to put these pies?" he asked.

Mr. Raymond kept his eyes on his cards and pointed to the desk. "I was in the mood for pizza. What are you? Some kind of a mind reader, Theo?"

Before Theo had a chance to answer, Lindsay marched over with a couple of pies. Pretending to fumble, she flipped opened the box and let the pizzas slip onto several of the men's laps. A moment later, Alex tossed his pie on Mr. Raymond and Theo.

And with that, a sudden flash of fur flew across the room. Ferdinand leapt in the air while Joker hung on for dear life. The dog landed on the table and reared back on his hind legs with Joker grasping hold of his collar as if he were riding a horse. He waved little Emilio high above his head as Ferdinand's front paws rose to the heavens. They made a mad dash for the other end of the table where Ferdinand locked onto a slice of pizza. He shook his head like a wild animal and ripped it apart.

Alex's jaw dropped. He stepped back just as the men shot up from their seats and threw their cards down.

"You joke?" Vlad glared hard at Mr. Raymond. He looked at the hot mess on his pants then shot the dog a fierce look. Ferdinand's body stiffened. He dropped the pizza, pulled back his lips, and bared his tiny white teeth. All at once, he lunged forward and grabbed the gold watch from the table.

"Why you miserable mongrel!" the man in the sunglasses sneered. He hunched his shoulders and tried to sneak behind Ferdinand.

"Hold on. I'll git 'im!" the man in the cowboy hat yelled. He removed his hat and slowly held it just above Ferdinand.

That's when the man in the baseball cap pounced.

In a moment of total chaos, Ferdinand jumped from the table with the watch dangling from his teeth. Theo and the four men chased after him as he darted wildly from the hallway into the kitchen and back again. They tried to tackle him, and each time, he managed to slip away.

Alex and Lindsay scrambled under the poker table, trying to avoid attention. They pushed the pizzas around pretending they were cleaning up the mess when Mr. Raymond got up from his chair. He stormed into the bathroom and turned on the light. "Kids these days are stupider than grass," he grunted and slammed the door behind him.

Alex shot up once the door closed. His eyes locked like magnets on his friends scattered between stacks of poker chips, money, and jewels. His fingers trembled as he pulled out the replacement deck and spread them along the edge of the table.

A fight broke out in the kitchen. The men raised their voices and pounded their fists on the counter, but Alex tried to stay focused. He repeated his father's words to himself, "Breathe life into it, and the magic will come."

"The magic will come!" he whispered and threw his arms in the air.

A sharp tingle coursed through the tips of his fingers. Across the entire table, poker chips rattled and cards quivered. He turned his palms upward, and the cards rose. They hung there, suspended above the table until Alex thrust his entire body into a sweeping gesture. In one fluid movement, his friends united, hovering like a school of fish just above the new deck. Alex spun his hand in a circular motion. He snapped his fingers and jumped back.

The Dance of Suits began.

The King swooped down and grabbed hold of his twin from the replacement deck. Just behind him, Queen Olivia—ever so gracefully—took her double from the table and joined the King. Spinning and turning, they dove beneath the light then spiraled up again. Jack soon followed. He grabbed his double— first tilting forward, to the side, then back. Gliding along, just the way Penelope showed him, he lengthened his stride as he looped above the table.

Lindsay stumbled backward with a look of utter disbelief on her face as, one by one, the cards assembled and took to the air. Hearts whirled above Diamonds. Clubs twirled beside Spades. They danced and swirled at Alex's command until a magnificent clutter filled the room. Specks of sunlight flickered across their tiny faces. They spiraled to the ceiling then back onto the green felt. With a turn of Alex's wrist, the replacement deck was carefully displayed right where the men had left their cards.

One at a time, his cherished friends whirled across the table into the palm of his hand. He held them tight and rushed toward the door.

"Wait!" the Queen shouted, pointing across the room. "What about Jack!"

Alex paused. He followed the Queen's gaze to the other side of the table where Jack stood as if he were frozen.

Alex leaned close. "Jack!" he whispered.

But Jack didn't budge. He just stared at Alex with a look of terror glued on his face.

Alex glanced around. The bathroom door was closed. The other men were in the kitchen. Lindsay was nowhere to be found. It was only a matter of seconds before the men convened at the poker table. Alex had to get out of there—fast!

He turned to Jack. "We have to go. NOW!"

Jack nodded frantically. He closed his eyes and tried to concentrate. He started to rise but quickly tumbled back to the table.

The men's voices grew louder. Alex inched toward the door— each step taking him farther from Jack.

He peered into the kitchen. The men were huddled in a circle by the sink. They had just started back into the room when Lindsay emerged. She handed the watch back to Vlad. Her overly-chatty explanation as to how the dog dropped it before it ran off seemed to fall on deaf ears. She glanced at Alex, her eyes wide with fear, pleading with him to hurry up!

Alex's heart raced. He shot around and shouted, "Jack! Let's go!"

Vlad stood in the doorway. He shook the watch, checking to make sure it still worked properly. Suddenly, the bathroom doorknob jiggled.

Mr. Raymond! Alex broke into a sweat. He reached his hand out one last time. "Jack—now!"

Alex calmed his nerves and gave one last turn of his wrist. Jack peeled himself off the green felt. His eyes on Alex, he slowly rose and began to spin, gradually picking up enough speed to twirl high above the table in tight circles. Jack landed in the middle of Alex's hand at the same moment the men charged back into the room. Alex slipped Jack deep in his pocket just as the men brushed past.

No one noticed Alex and Lindsay sneaked out of the room. Not even Mr. Raymond. He marched from the bathroom, his shirt and pants soggy and stained, right back to the poker table.

It was abundantly clear as he settled in beside the pile of money and jewelry before him, all he cared about was winning. Alex paused in the hallway. He took one last look as Mr. Raymond lit a cigar, picked up his cards, and grinned at the men. He even offered to treat them to another lunch, just as long as they sat back down and finished the game. And they obliged.

But this time, everything was different.

Slip Up

Lindsay stared at Alex as if he were a ghost.

He ran his fingers over his face to make sure nothing was hanging from his nose. "What's the matter?"

"You— your—those cards—they really are—magic!"

Alex smiled. "I tried to tell you."

"Yeah, but how—"

"There's the hot dog guy. You want one?" Alex interrupted.

Lindsay stood there scratching her head. Ferdinand yanked his leash and pulled Alex into the park beside a brilliant red oak tree.

"Unless of course you'd rather have pizza!" he teased.

"Very funny." Lindsay squinted. "I'll get in line."

With a few moments alone, Alex set his sights on the nearest bench. Shoulders hunched, he tucked himself in the corner and pulled his cards from his pocket.

Before he could blink, the King gave a snap and hopped on the bench. "Well, that was quite an adventure!"

"I must admit, the overnight accommodations were lovely," the Queen followed.

"I promise I'll never leave you on a table again to go off and sign some silly autograph!"

"Alex," the King said, "you didn't do anything wrong. That could have happened to anyone. You're a talented magician. You have a right to enjoy your successes in life." He smiled warmly as the rest of the suits jumped onto the bench beside him. "Something tells me winning that contest was just the beginning!"

Alex felt himself breathe for the first time. Just listening to their little voices, he realized how much he had missed them. They whispered and laughed and celebrated how perfectly well The Dance came together. Suddenly, he noticed Jack was not taking part. Alex glanced at the other end of the bench. Jack was standing alone with a troubled look on his face.

"What's wrong?" Alex asked.

"I have to go back," Jack answered.

"Back where?"

"To that poker place."

"What?"

"Penelope's still in the safe."

"Who's Penelope?"

"She's a charm. A beautiful, sweet, golden charm. And she's been trapped in Mr. Raymond's safe for too long. I have to get her out. You've got to help me, Alex."

Alex looked beyond the park in the direction of the Cider Shoppe and shut his eyes. Just the thought of going back there made his stomach turn. "Jack, I—"

"Please, Alex. I know we can do this. Please help me!"

Alex held his head in his hands and moaned to himself. He had never seen Jack this upset. Even so, he couldn't help but feel like this was yet another huge mistake he was about to make. He slipped Jack in his pocket. But this time, he wasn't going to take any chances with the rest of his cards.

He rushed over to Lindsay. "I really need your help. Can you take these cards back to my house where they'll be safe? Please?

The back door is open. Just hang out there with Ferdinand until
I get back, okay?"

"I don't understand. Didn't we get everything?"

"Not exactly. I'll explain later," Alex said as he sprinted away.

The parade was in full swing as they hurried through the
crowded streets to the Cider Shoppe and once again slipped
down the alleyway. Alex looked up and noticed the window ajar.
He hoisted himself onto the garbage can and slowly raised his
eyes over the sill.

He blinked a few times, stunned by the drastic turn of events.
The mountain of poker chips, jewels, and money that had been
heaped before Mr. Raymond was now dispersed among the
other gamblers. Mr. Raymond squirmed in his chair.

"Good! He's lost everything," Jack whispered. He hopped on
the sill and lay down on his back. "Can you manage that sleight
of hand move and swing me over by the safe?"

Alex studied Jack's card, then the window. The space was
tight. There was hardly enough room to maneuver his wrist
between the bars. "Jack, I'm never going to be able to get you
over to the safe without being seen!"

Jack looked straight at Alex. "I thought you magicians never
say 'never'!"

Alex smiled.

No sooner had Jack repeated Alex's own words, when Mr.
Raymond got up from his chair and shuffled beside the safe. He
gave a heavy sigh and turned the combination.

"Alex. We have to do it NOW!" Jack said.

Alex didn't have time to think. He thrust his hand between
the bars and twisted his wrist until it burned. He flung Jack with
such force that he cut through the air and landed on the safe

without anyone noticing. With a quick snap, Jack jumped up and scurried out of sight.

Mr. Raymond's face turned a grayish-green color as he opened the safe. He stood up straight, tucked his chin in his neck, and let out a colossal belch. "Get me some cider!" he said, searching for Theo. "I'm having one of my episodes."

Jack slid behind the safe door and peeked inside. Penelope was quivering in her velvet pouch. Her muffled charms chattered beneath her. Mr. Raymond grabbed the pouch and placed it on top of the safe. When he reached in again, Jack leapt up and grasped the pouch by its cord. He hoisted it over his shoulder, planted his feet, and looked straight at Alex. Once their eyes locked, Alex twisted his wrist, summoning Jack to return. Jack began to spin across the room. With Penelope in tow, he landed on the sill and climbed through the bars back into Alex's hand. Mr. Raymond, still digging around in the safe, pulled out the last of the bills and shut the door. But when he reached for the bracelet pouch . . .

"Who took the bracelet?" Mr. Raymond bellowed, his voice traveling through the brick walls of the poker den, into the Cider Shoppe, and along the narrow alleyway. Still, the gamblers remained seated, unfazed by his thunderous outburst.

"Who—stole—my—gold bracelet?" he screamed.

Each man glanced at the other. They all stood up and gathered around him.

"Are you accusin' us of stealin'?" the man in the cowboy hat leaned close.

"Uhhh." Mr. Raymond stepped back.

"Don't even think about getting outta this one!" the man in the dark sunglasses said.

"Da!" Vlad agreed. He placed his arm around Mr. Raymond and escorted him back to his seat. "Is humble opinion, you finish game."

Alex peered through the window one last time as Mr. Raymond mopped his head with his handkerchief. It suddenly seemed worth a second trip just to see the twisted look on his face when he shrank in his chair.

Alex tucked Jack in his pocket. "Mission accomplished!" He turned to leave, but just as he was about to jump off the garbage can, he lost his balance. He hit the ground. The pouch went flying and the can crashed onto the cobblestone with a resounding metallic thud. Alex held his breath. He sat on the cold stone with his eyes shut, praying no one heard the steel can rocking back and forth. After a painfully long moment, the can settled, and everything turned still. He got on his knees and reached for the pouch when the oddest feeling came over him. It felt like someone was watching him. He raised his eyes up the brick wall to the window. There was Mr. Raymond. His face was glowing red, and his massive fist was pressed against the glass. Theo appeared by his side. "That's the kid!" he shouted. "The one who did those card tricks!"

Alex shuddered. He jumped to his feet and raced toward the street, clutching the velvet pouch.

Mr. Raymond's voice echoed through the alleyway. "Get him! Now! That magic kid stole my bracelet!"

An Apple a Day

The Granny Smith Apple Cloggers were just about to shuffle up Main Street when Alex flew by. Irish music filled the air as row after row of silver-haired grandmas stood raring to go. They tapped their toes and hopped in place, shooting up and down like popcorn in a hot pan.

Alex weaved his way between the dancers and pushed deeper into the parade. Every few seconds, he glanced over his shoulder, hoping he wasn't being chased. With his attention behind him, he stumbled into a pack of clowns. They clomped along in oversized shoes and squeaked their silvery horns. One of them grabbed Alex by the shoulders and held him close to his face. His thick white makeup and wiry orange hair startled him.

"Be careful, son. You don't want to get hurt," he said.

Alex jumped back.

"Look! Behind you!" Jack shouted, leaning out of Alex's back pocket.

Alex swung around just as Theo blasted through the alleyway. He skidded to a halt in the middle of the grandmas' dance routine. He ducked and dodged as they merrily kicked him along in their wooden-soled shoes.

Alex kept running. He broke into a sweat, hurrying past the smiling faces of hundreds of happy onlookers. They packed the streets cheering and waving their little flags, but all he could think of was his horrible luck. In his effort to help Jack, not only was he officially a thief, he was officially a thief being chased through the only event he wanted absolutely nothing to do with. Things couldn't get much worse.

He darted past the Little Lady Apple Twirlers spinning their shiny batons and quickly found himself marching alongside the 45th Infantry Band. Outfitted in their burgundy and gold braided uniforms, their horns rang out as their shoulders swayed from side to side.

"Hurry!" Jack yelled.

Alex turned back. Theo was limping at a pretty fast clip. His eyes roamed the crowd like an animal on the hunt.

Alex dropped below the bass drum. Its deep thumps vibrated through his brain as he tried to figure out a way to get to the next float without being spotted. He glanced back at the Little Lady Apple Twirlers. They had just launched their batons in the air when Theo came bursting through like a cannonball. He stumbled into the last row of twirlers who fell into the next row. All of which collided into a red sequined heap. Seconds later, their batons dropped from the skies, one by one onto Theo's head.

Alex shot through a row of trombone players and zigzagged his way through the line. He had almost reached the next float when someone in the bleachers shouted his name.

"Alexander Finn! Is that you?"

Alex cringed. It was Mrs. Fardull, the singing, coin-disappearing cowgirl's mother from the magic contest. She waved her arm like a beauty queen. Not wanting to be rude, Alex nodded. Then he swung around, hoping Theo hadn't heard her.

"Do you see her?" She pointed excitedly. "That's my little Dee-Dee up there!"

Alex turned to the float. Swathed in layers of rose-colored netting, ten little girls—each perched on a fake tree stump—waved to the crowd beneath a canopy brimming with tiny apple blossoms. Way in the back row was Dee-Dee. Her tiara slipped down her face each time the float hit a bump.

"Congratulations!" Alex shouted.

"Run, Alex, please!" Jack yelled.

Theo shoved the trombone players aside. Their notes turned sour as he passed. Alex crouched low to the ground. The midday sun beat on his face as he squinted ahead. He wondered how long he could keep running before he ran out of places to hide. With just a few floats left, he needed to come up with a better plan.

He was searching for a gap in the bleachers that he could slip through when something smacked his cheek. There was Dylan, standing in the front row with a straw hanging from his bottom lip. At once, the whole football team stood. As the marching band roared by, they all did the wiggle dance in time to the music.

Alex was mortified. He was beginning to think bad luck was just his fate when an idea popped into his head. "Dylan!" Alex shouted, waving him over.

Dylan lowered his straw and look at him curiously. He jumped off the bleacher and sprinted to his side.

"You see that guy back there in the Hawaiian shirt?" Alex said, trying to appear calm.

Dylan craned his neck then turned back to Alex. "Uh-huh."

"I heard he's taking over for Mr. Schnitzer. He's getting rid of the football team."

Dylan's eyes turned to slits. He gave Alex the thumbs up and circled back to his friends in the bleachers.

Seconds later, a barrage of spitballs launched in the air. Alex turned back as the boys aimed their straws at Theo like Amazon tribesmen about to shoot poisonous darts. Theo scrambled for cover. He tripped and rolled on the ground just as the trombone players marched by. They stepped over him, hoisting their legs as if they were climbing over a log.

Alex raced ahead. Sweat ran down his face and dripped off his nose and chin like tears. He flew past the roller-skating flute players and the colorful mimes on their tiny red scooters. Confetti fluttered like snowflakes in the wind as he ran by a procession of vintage cars. The windows were rolled down and the uniformed drivers tipped their hats at the crowd. Alex grabbed onto the passenger side of a gloss-black Model T. He was about to leap into the back seat when he pictured Theo poking his face inside the car window. Alex became frantic. His eyes bounced from the car, to the float ahead, then back to Theo whose twisted face kept reappearing in and out of the crowd.

"Run, Alex, run!" Jack screamed.

Alex leaped from the car and shot ahead. He grabbed onto the side of the float, flung his leg up, and rolled out of sight.

Theo was in plain view. With his all too familiar gape, he charged forward, thrusting the mimes to one side and their scooters in the other direction. He moved closer, shoving his head in each of the vintage cars. Alex gasped as Theo ran his finger alongside the Model T then slowly raised his eyes in his direction.

Heart banging, his shirt soaked with sweat, Alex squirmed backward and crashed against a pile of hay. He swung around and peered over the hay at a group of teenagers who were preparing to bob for apples. They slipped on their plastic ponchos, got to their knees, and lowered their heads. Poised and ready to go, a bell sounded. The crowd along the street whistled and clapped as the teens dunked their faces in the sloshing tub of water.

"He's coming!" Jack screamed.

Alex turned. Theo was just behind the float. With seconds left, he scrambled between the teens and plunged his face into the tub. The frigid water hit him like a brick.

Everything turned to a frozen hum. His heart banging against his chest was all he heard. It thumped so loud the water shook every time it took a beat. Alex knelt there, hoping to wait it out. Then it dawned on him—he had no way to gauge where Theo was. For all he knew he was limping right beside the float waiting for him to pop up for air. He tried not to think about it, or the fact that his ears had gone completely numb. Instead, Alexander Finn tried to remain calm. And so, to distract himself, he began to count.

Ninety-nine, ninety-eight, ninety-seven. The longer he counted, the harder his head throbbed. *Ninety-four, ninety-three, ninety-two.* His eyeballs felt like ice cubes. *Eighty-four, eighty-three! Have–to–hold–on–one–more . . . eighty-two.* His lungs began to burn. *Another second, another second, one more second!* He jumped up, gasping for air, just as the back of Theo's head passed by. Inches from Alex's frozen face, Theo scanned the crowd.

With his sopping wet hair dripping down his shirt and the worst brain freeze ever, Alex shook his head like a dog. He jumped off the float and ran in the opposite direction. Icy water streamed down his neck as he cut across the parade and down a side street. He turned back every so often just to be sure Theo was far off his trail.

Finally, Alex reached a quiet corner, where he collapsed against a mailbox to catch his breath.

"We did it!" Jack shouted. "We really did it!"

Alex straightened. His chest heaved, his legs trembled, but he still managed a smile. Just as he reached in his pocket for Jack, someone grabbed him from behind and yanked him off his feet. Alex dug his fingers deep into the man's powerful hands.

"Well, well, what have we here? If it isn't the champ." Mr. Raymond snarled as he dragged him toward the bushes.

"Let me go!" Alex choked.

Mr. Raymond spun him around and raised him close to his face. "Perhaps I'll let you go when you give me back my bracelet." His eyes turned to narrow slits as he tightened his grip. "I don't think you want to know what happens to magicians who get caught stealing from me. . . . Do you?"

Alex stared into his eyes. They were evil eyes, like the wicked magician's in his dream. His body shook. His arms thrashed as he tried to kick, but it was no use. He was no match for Mr. Raymond's massive size.

Behind them, the apple float had just reached the corner. The horses began to turn when the wheel hit the curb. Bushel after bushel of apples rocked and tottered each time the float tried to maneuver the corner.

"I'm not going to ask you again." Mr. Raymond twisted Alex's collar tighter.

Alex could barely breathe. He hung there, inches off the ground, his bulging eyes fixed on the horses. Their hooves clomped madly as they struggled forward. Alex threw his hand behind him. His fingers clawed their way into his pants pocket until he finally reached the edge of Jack's card. Choking and wheezing, he slowly inched him out.

His shoulders were wedged up by his ears, but Alex managed to bend his elbow, twisting his wrist until it burned. With all the strength he had left, he flung Jack, who spun wildly in place. He twirled to the right, looped to the left, and boomeranged in a tight circle, hitting Mr. Raymond directly in the eye.

Mr. Raymond's hands shot up to his face. He let out a piercing shrill. Alex collapsed on the ground, gasping for air at the same moment the apple float jumped the curb. Mr. Raymond stumbled aimlessly into the street just as the float capsized. An avalanche of apples—ninety-seven bushels to be exact—rolled off the float and buried him.

THE REAL DEAL

The next afternoon, Alex reached into one of the boxes piled against his wall and pulled out his lacrosse awards. He wiped them with his T-shirt then placed them on the shelf next to his magic trophy.

Lindsay had just finished hanging his father's Houdini poster above the bed when she turned and said, "Wow! Those trophies look really cool together!"

"Check this out," Alex said, reaching in his pocket. He turned to Ferdinand and held up a treat. The dog perked up and started to pant. "Okay," Alex sang. "Show Lindsay what we practiced." Alex stirred his finger clockwise, and the dog leaped into a somersault. He stirred the opposite direction, and the dog rolled over and sat on his hind legs with his paws raised. "Good Boy!" Alex said. He tossed a biscuit in the air and Ferdinand caught it with his teeth. "Ta-da!"

"I'm impressed!" Lindsay clapped. "Maybe you should include Ferdinand in your magic act!"

Alex laughed. "Not a bad idea."

"Jeez, I hardly recognize this place," Alex's mom said, poking her head in his room.

"Ha-ha." Alex joked.

"Take a look." She beamed, holding the newspaper in front of her. "Thanks to you, my article made the front page!"

Bold letters ran across the top: "Cider Shoppe Owner—One Bad Apple!"

Alex took the paper from her. "FBI Nabs Six in High Stakes Poker Scam."

"Hey! You're a local hero!" Lindsay said, peeking over his shoulder.

"Well, Dylan too. He spitballed Theo right into the hands of the police!"

Alex scrolled down the page. Just below the article was his photograph. He was handing the gold charm bracelet back to its rightful owner—Mr. Peter Diller.

His mom grabbed him by the shoulders. "You did the right thing, you know. Your father would have been very proud."

Alex sighed. "I never meant to keep it." He stepped over to the desk and gazed out the window. It suddenly dawned on him how close he had come to some real-life criminals, and how much danger he had put himself and Lindsay in. It seemed so surreal, just like in the movies—all the way through the big chase.

"Well, I have to say, it was rather nice of Mr. Diller to let you keep one of those charms," she said. "Which one did you choose?"

Alex smiled. His eyes lowered onto the little ballerina poised on the sill. Penelope blew him a kiss just as Jack stepped over and took her hand.

Alex's attention turned to the family across the street. They were lugging pumpkins up the steps to their front door. Their two boys turned and waved. Alex gave a nod and waved back. "Have you ever hated something so much, then had it change your life . . . you know, in a good way?"

His mom stepped beside him. "From time to time. Funny how that works, isn't it?"

"Yeah." He grinned.

She ran her hand through his hair then turned to leave. "Oh! I just remembered, there's one more bit of news. It seems the mayor is planning a special commendation in your honor. It's sort of like a civilian service award." She raised her brow. "It's a pretty big deal, honey."

Alex turned. "For what?"

She pulled out her memo pad, "For, and I quote, Alexander Finn's outstanding contribution to the well-being of the community of Orchard." She paused as she headed for the door. "Oh, and one more thing. He wants you to be the grand marshal on the Orchard float next year."

Alex's jaw dropped. He rushed after her into the hallway and watched her dance down the stairs.

"Gotcha!" she shouted.

"Mom, that's not even funny!"

It was dusk by the time Alex and Lindsay finished arranging his room. Once the last box was emptied, Alex took a long look around. Houdini and Kellar posters now hung above his bed. Across the room, books and treasured trophies lined the shelves. For the first time, it felt like home.

"So, I hear they're having a magic contest at the library next month," Lindsay said. "You should totally sign up!"

"I'd like that," Alex said. He reached for his cards, studied them for a moment then ran his fingers across their edge. "Did I ever tell you about the curious butterfly?"

Lindsay smiled and took a seat on the edge of his bed.

Alex placed two cards side by side. He moved them through the air as if they were flapping wings. Their shadows jumped across his wall as they rose and fell. He snapped his fingers, and the cards vanished. In their place, a brilliant blue and ochre butterfly fluttered. Its iridescent wings caught the light and shimmered as it circled the room and landed on his finger. It lingered for a moment then zigzagged over the desk and out into the evening sky.

Alex and Lindsay rushed to the window and watched it disappear.

"That was amazing! How did you do that?"

Alex laid the cards beside him and gazed out at the purple night. His thoughts traveled back to their old kitchen and his last conversation with his dad. His father's words filled his heart. "I don't know." Alex smiled. "It just popped into my head—as if it was always there—like an old friend."

Joker slipped on his new lime green silk jacket. "Wait a minute! This isn't what I ordered. I'm a winter! I can't wear this! I'll look . . . sickly."

King Anton marched over to his Queen's side and folded his arms. "Thank goodness that's over."

"Pardon?" the Queen said.

The King cleared his throat. "I said, 'See! Everything worked out fine.' Just as I predicted, all it takes is a bit of patience!" He tipped his crown back on his head and leaned a little closer. "Did you hear the one about the magician?"

She wrinkled her brow. "No."

"He was walking down the street and turned into a grocery store!"

Queen Olivia smiled. She reached over to kiss him on the cheek but paused when she noticed the King's face went pale. His attention had shifted to the opposite side of the desk. He was staring hard at the photograph of Alex's father.

"What's wrong?" she asked.

Alex turned. "Is something wrong?"

"Did you see that?" the King asked.

Alex and the Queen leaned close. "See what?"

"For a minute there, I thought"—the King rubbed his eyes and looked again—"I could have sworn the Incredible Finn just winked at me!"

Alex grabbed the photograph off the desk and held it in the evening light. "DAD?"

ABOUT THE AUTHOR

Laurie Smollett Kutscera was born in Greenwich Village and grew up in Queens, New York. She performed her first magic trick at age 11 and was destined to be a ventriloquist with the aid of her childhood friend, Neil, who remains a real magician today. Rather than follow in the footsteps of Houdini, she went on to study fine art and children's book illustration at Queens College with Caldecott medalist Marvin Bileck. She is an award-winning graphic designer, a published children's book illustrator, and toy designer.

Laurie's passion for writing began 12 years ago while cruising the eastern seaboard from Nantucket to the Virgin Islands. Today she continues to write and illustrate and is currently working on several contemporary picture books and middle grade novels.

Laurie lives on the North Shore of Long Island with her husband Nick and rescue dog, Cody. You can learn more about Laurie by going to lskillustration.com.

CPSIA information can be obtained
at www.ICGtesting.com
Printed in the USA
LVHW042354280420
654643LV00003B/57